The Third Brother

Nick McDonell is 21 years old and was born in New York City.
He is a student at Harvard University.

ALSO BY NICK McDONELL

Twelve

The Third Brother

Nick McDonell

Atlantic Books
London

First published in 2005 in the United States of America by Grove Press, an imprint of Grove/Atlantic, Inc.

First published in Great Britain in trade paperback in 2006 by Atlantic Books, an imprint of Grove Atlantic Ltd.

This paperback edition published in 2006 by Atlantic Books.

9 8 7 6 5 4 3 2 1

A CIP catalogue record for this book is available from the British Library.

ISBN 10: 1 84354 478 4
ISBN 13: 978 1 84354 478 4

Printed in Great Britain

Atlantic Books
An imprint of Grove Atlantic Ltd
Ormond House
26–27 Boswell Street
London WC1N 3JZ

To my mother

The Third Brother

PART I

Mike was privileged and troubled at the same time. He knew that if you grow up with money you don't think about being rich, and that the same is probably true of courage. But if you grow up with lies, you find out that some lies become true. Mike knew this, too, and so did not lie. Except to himself, about his parents.

They were husband and wife but sometimes mistaken for siblings. They could have been carved out of the same piece of alabaster. Mike inherited the long high planes of their cheekbones, and he loved his parents in a very conscious way. They were both troubled themselves, and their trouble accelerated Mike's childhood. He had seen them at their worst, violent and irrational, naked in public, smooth features contorted. In his reckoning as a young man, though, they were fine, and he had decided, in the face of their madness and addictions, that he loved them. And his life was his own.

1

The summer is dragging for Mike as he rises, by escalator, out of the cool subway into the Hong Kong heat. He is too tall, out of place as he crosses the jammed street to Taikoo Tower, where he has been working for six weeks. Seems like a year. The tower looms over him, silent workers and pulsing technology, a kingdom of itself above the Hong Kong streets. Mike doesn't like the skyscraper—it has become predictable—but he is grateful for the air-conditioning. Everything inside the tower works. Outside, not. His job, his internship, is at a news magazine that he had never read until the twenty-two-hour flight from New York.

Mike has several bosses at the magazine, but the reason he has the job is that the managing editor, Elliot Analect, is a friend of his father. Analect even looks like his father, Mike realized when they shook hands. All of those guys look alike, all tall, clean, white guys who have known one another for decades. They were in the same club at Harvard, wore the same ties. And then they went to Vietnam and almost all of them came back. Growing up, Mike didn't see his father's friends much but he had the sense they were in touch. So when it was time for his first internship, the summer after his freshman year, Mike was not surprised that he ended up working for Analect. He was glad, at least, that the job was in Hong Kong and not in midtown Manhattan.

As a summer intern, Mike seldom gets out of the office, spends his days wading the Internet. He is doing research, mostly for Thomas Bishop, one of the magazine's correspondents. Mike has a view of Analect's office and sometimes watches his father's old friend through the smoked-glass walls, but they have had little contact since that initial welcome handshake. And the most excitement Mike has had was when Analect abruptly spoke with him in the hallway, promising to take him out to lunch at the end of the summer. Strange, Mike thinks, and wishes there was more for him to do. As he surfs the Internet he thinks about fathers and sons, and how friendship does not necessarily pass down. Mike has already seen this often among his friends and their fathers.

So Mike is glad when the assignment comes, even though he is very surprised. He had been watching again, and Analect had been standing in conversation with Bishop for nearly ten minutes. Mike had been looking closely through the glass—he sensed the men were angry with one another—when Bishop suddenly turned and opened the door. Mike feared he was caught, but then Bishop waved him into the office and Analect asked if he wanted to go to Bangkok. "Help Tommy with some reporting," as he put it.

Bishop nods slightly at Mike. Bishop is a small man, with fat features and prematurely graying black hair.

"The story is backpacker kids going to Bangkok to do ecstasy," Analect says. "Just don't get arrested."

"He doesn't want to have to retrieve you," Bishop says.

"It's really just a travel story, is another way to look at it," Analect goes on.

"Just a travel story," Bishop repeats, chuckling.

"You're their age," Analect continues, "the backpackers'. You'll be good at talking to them. Ask questions. It can be your story too. And one other thing I've already explained to Tommy . . ."

Mike catches Bishop rolling his eyes.

". . . I want you to find Christopher Dorr."

Mike can't place the name.

"He used to do a lot of the investigative pieces Tommy does now," Analect says, looking straight at him, seeming almost to ignore Bishop. "He's been in Bangkok for a while, I think. It'd be good for someone from the magazine to look him up."

Mike tries to decode this and can't. Analect tells him again to stay out of trouble and that Bishop will take care of him. It seems to Mike that Bishop is pleased to have the help, but that there is more to it. When they are leaving the office, Analect tells Mike to wait for a moment, and when they are alone, he tells Mike that Dorr had been a friend of Mike's father, years ago. That they had all been good friends, actually, the three of them practically brothers, and that Mike's father would be glad for news of Dorr.

Mike looks out the window. He notices for the first time how really extraordinary the view from Analect's office is. Mike can see the whole city, enormous and smogged and throbbing. For a moment he can't believe the sound of it doesn't blow in the windows. But Analect's office sits quietly above it all, humming coolly. Mike is suddenly uneasy, with only the inch of glass between the two of them and the loud, empty space above the city. He looks back at Analect, who is frowning.

"Dorr and your father were sparring partners, when they boxed back in college," says Analect.

Mike looks back out over the city. He knew about the boxing, but his father had never mentioned Dorr. It all surprises him, but maybe it's just seeing his own features reflected in the glass, and the long drop to Hong Kong from fifty stories up.

2

When Mike was a small boy, his parents often entertained. In New York City in their world, they were famous for the dinners they gave in their big beach house at the end of Long Island, especially Thanksgiving. Mike remembered the candlelight and gluey cranberry sauce, which he would wipe off his hands into his hair. His older brother, Lyle, remembered the same things. There were servants, who disciplined Mike when his parents did not. One Filipino lady in particular boxed his ears. When he was older he remembered how it hurt but not her name. Their parents gave these dinners several years in a row. There were mostly the same guests, adults who would tousle Mike's fine but cranberried hair, and their children, a crew of beautiful, spoiled playmates whom Mike assumed he would know forever. He still saw some of them, at parties and dinners of their own on school breaks. At hearing that one or two of them had slid into addiction, Mike would remember chasing them through his mother's busy kitchen. His mother was never in the kitchen, of course, but it was definitely hers. Small paintings of vegetables and an antique mirror hung on its walls.

When dinner started, the children would go to the playroom and eat with the nannies. They lounged on overstuffed couches, watching movies until they fell asleep and the nannies went outside for cigarettes. Lyle especially loved these dinners and made a point of talking to everybody, lingering in the dining room rather than watching movies with the other children. He loved listening to adults talk. So did Mike, but he knew he didn't understand the way his older brother did.

The adults sat and drank wine and laughed and smiled at one another in the fall candlelight. Many of them had started families late or had been married once before and had only recently started new ones. Jobs were interesting; there was much travel. There was a lot to talk about, and the subtext was that they were lucky to have the lives they had. Mike remembered everyone being very happy.

Before one of these dinners, Lyle decided that he and Mike would be spies. Lyle had gotten a small tape recorder, only a toy really, for his birthday earlier that fall. Their plan was to hide it in the dining room to record the dinner conversation. While the servants were setting up, and Mike's mother was upstairs dressing and Mike's father was out walking along the ocean, Lyle and Mike secured the tape recorder under the table with duct tape.

As the guests arrived and had drinks, the boys slid between them and crawled under the table and switched on the recorder.

They were very excited all through dinner, but they didn't tell any of the other children what they were up to. By dessert, Mike couldn't wait any longer. He wanted to go get the recorder. No, said Lyle, they'll be there for a long time. Let's just look.

When they peeked around the dining room door, Elliot Analect saw them and held up the tape recorder, which he must have found much earlier, maybe when he first sat down. Analect wasn't a regular guest at these dinners. He was usually abroad somewhere. At that point he was a correspondent in East Asia, and Mike's father was especially glad to have him for Thanksgiving. Mike's mother didn't like Analect. Mike didn't know this the way Lyle did, but he had a sense of it too.

When Analect held up the recorder Mike knew instantly they would be in trouble. He saw the way the adults laughed but didn't think it was funny. One of them, drunker than the rest and not a very good friend of Mike's parents, was even a little angry. Mike remembered that he worked for one of the networks. Their mother was embarrassed and that always made her cross as well. Mike's father called the boys over and tried to set things right by giving them a talk, in front of everyone, that was both funny and serious. Analect removed the tape from the recorder and put it in his pocket.

3

On the flight from HKI to BKK, Mike asks Bishop about Christopher Dorr.

"A crazy fuck," Bishop tells him. "Won awards. Then just stopped filing, so the magazine stopped paying him. I won't bullshit you, I never liked the guy much."

Mike doesn't know what to say.

"Analect's the one that lost him," Bishop goes on. "He should check in on Dorr himself."

Mike looks out the window at the flat turquoise sea below. He wonders if Analect has spoken to his father since he arrived in Hong Kong. No, or his father would have said something. But then they haven't talked much since Mike left. Mike knows there were some things his father never talked about. His life before his children wasn't a secret; it just never came up. Mike always thought that maybe this was because his father hadn't wanted to end up in banking but did anyway. Mike thinks if he talks to Dorr he'll know a lot more about that.

"You don't have to worry about Dorr," Bishop is saying. "Just fill your notebook with stony backpacker quotes and we'll have a week in Bangkok. Pretty girls in Bangkok. You'll have a blast."

Mike keeps expecting Bishop to give him specifics about what else he wants for the story but he never does, just sleeps most of the three-hour ride. Mike looks at Bishop and thinks that if you sleep on a plane you could crash and be unsure whether you are dreaming until you are dead. Mike isn't worried about the specifics. He figures he'll get whatever information he needs when the time comes. Bishop has already told him they'd have the place wired because of some friends of his who are based in Bangkok.

"You'll like them," Bishop said, and then called them the "flying circus."

Following Bishop, Mike sails through Bangkok customs on a tourist visa. The room is hot but the lines are short. Customs officials in lizard-colored uniforms slam their stamps, and the pale Europeans and Americans in bright, patterned shirts sweat in line and shuffle through.

As they clear, Bishop tells Mike that in Bangkok it's easier to be a journalist if you're not a journalist. "You'll see what I mean when you meet the flying circus," he says. "They get away with anything."

On the way in from the airport, Bishop tells Mike to take the night off, check out the city. He is going to meet his "best girl" and, in fact, is going to be spending most of his time with her. He needs a break. This is good for Mike because he will get to do most of the reporting. Of course Bishop will write the story in the end; Mike just has to find the stony quotes. They both get a week in Bangkok and he will make sure they share the byline. "It'll be a good surprise for Analect, but you really have to do it yourself," says Bishop.

Getting out of the cab in front of their hotel, Mike knows that Bishop is going to ditch him. What the hell.

4

Mike knew something strange and probably bad had happened that Thanksgiving. Everyone went home earlier than usual. Lyle was miserable, almost in tears, and Mike tried to comfort him. Mike often felt that he did not see problems his older brother saw.

As the two boys lay in their bunks that night, Lyle in the top, they heard the sounds of an argument coming from their parents' room across the hall. Eventually the sounds would become so familiar that Mike never remembered a time when he had not heard them, but this was one of the first times. Lyle climbed down to investigate. Where are you going? Mike asked, watching his brother's legs swing out into dark space. Lyle didn't answer, though, just crept across the hall and listened at his parents' door.

Mike pulled his covers up over his head and tensed his small body. Then he got out of bed and went across the hall too. He saw Lyle there, lying on the floor with his ear to the bottom of the door. Their parents were really yelling now and their voices seemed very loud in the hallway. Mike lay next to his brother and tried to listen, but Lyle pushed him away. Go to bed, Lyle said, in the way their parents often ordered.

Mike wouldn't go. They began to tussle but froze when they heard the argument stop. Their parents had heard them. Lyle grabbed Mike and they ran back to their beds. Their parents opened the door but didn't catch them.

Mike waited until his older brother fell asleep and then went and listened at his parents' door again. He couldn't tell what they were talking about, but he heard Analect's name. After that night he was always a little suspicious of Analect, although he could not say why, exactly.

5

The hotel is white with a revolving door. It is jammed in among the hostels on Khao San Road. As he is checking in, Mike overhears a paunchy Brit describing the hotel to his wife as "the best place to see Bangkok from the street." Mike doubts that. His room is on the third floor, small, with a shower and satellite television. A baseball game is on when he walks in. He looks out the window down the length of Khao San Road vibrating in the heat.

Across the street from the hotel is a row of cafés. They are all different, Italian, Thai, American, and so on, but they are really all the same, like everything else on Khao San Road. Mike figures that every backpacker in Southeast Asia starts and ends here. He sits down at the closest café and orders a beer, and a backpacker kid, twirling his dreadlocks around his ringed thumbs at the next table, asks him how it's going and joins him.

"Fine," says Mike, "how about you?"

"Good except the cops are fucking everywhere," says Dreads.

Mike hasn't seen any cops except those directing traffic.
"You just get here?" asks Dreads. Mike tells him yes and
then Dreads gives him three minutes on the wonders of Thailand. Getting high on the beaches, riding the elephants up
north, getting high on the elephant rides, dancing in the clubs.
This is exactly what Analect said would happen. It's easy for
Mike to talk to this kid, who keeps bragging about the club
he is going to later. Like any middle-class stoner from back
home, but somehow transformed by heat and distance into a
legitimate denizen of this strange locale. Mike thinks it's as
though someone dropped a tropical urban bomb on the mall
he slouched through every day.

"Want to come get fucked up?" he asks Mike.

So Mike goes to the club, Z Club it's called, and stays all night,
wondering at first if he is really working or just having another
green beer. It's a dance club, could have been London or Paris
or New York, where he's from, but Mike doesn't really know
because he doesn't go to clubs.

The strobes illuminate the dancers in smoky flashes, sun-
burned Europeans and black Africans so dark they almost disappear. Where are those guys from? Mike wonders. It's like
they're from the surface of the sun. Mike doesn't dance. He
stands at the crowded bar drinking beers, and then sometimes
he walks to the wall and leans there drinking, watching the sinu-
ous dancers. He is trying to pick up the signals, what is what,
trying to pick out the tourists from the locals. Easy. Tourists
talk to him because he looks like them. A South African relates

how a woman shot a dart out of her pussy the night before at a club in Patpong.

Three dumpy Kiwi girls pull him to a couch and talk to him about how cheap everything is in Thailand and how much they like it that foreigners come up and talk to them. In the end they tell him he's cute and they'll look him up when they get to New York at the end of their holiday. At first Mike thinks maybe this would be fine. Maybe he wants to fuck one of these girls, or even all three at once. But not really. He has a girlfriend, Jane, back home, and that was complicated enough already. Plus he is working, isn't he?

6

During his freshman year, Mike sometimes studied in a wing of Widener Library named after the nineteenth-century historian Robert Benson Ames. The name meant nothing to Mike when Analect told him to look up Christopher Dorr, but then it did because on the Internet he found out that Dorr's full name was Christopher Ames Dorr. Mike wondered if the two were related. Probably, he figured.

Supposedly the Ames wing was haunted, and there was a tradition, a joke really, about making Phi Beta Kappa or something if you had sex there when you were a freshman. When Jane visited him over a long weekend that fall, he mentioned this to her and she said it sounded like a good tradition. Mike said he only mentioned it because it was so ridiculous, but then he was pleased when Jane insisted on seeing the library. After all, it was very old and very famous. So she and Mike walked through the stacks, talking in low voices as the motion sensors clicked and lit lamps above the rows of books they passed, until they found a place.

Jane froze while they were having sex. The light in the next aisle clicked on.

"Did you hear that?" she whispered.

Mike became very serious, as if he were almost expecting something.

"Breathing," said Jane. "But I didn't hear any footsteps."

She kept a straight face. Mike thought she might really be scared and he hurried to pull himself together. He even took her by the hand and started to lead her out of the aisle. When they were three rows away and hadn't said anything, Jane couldn't contain herself anymore. Her laughter overwhelmed the quiet of the library. "I knew it," she said. "You really thought there might be a ghost."

But Jane didn't get it. It's not that Mike believes in ghosts, it's that he knows you can be haunted.

7

By midnight, Dreads has a whole backpacker crew gathered around him, eyes flooding from the ecstasy. Mike watches them dance, bumping into one another, stopping only to pull beaten water bottles from the pockets of their cheap linen fisherman's pants, just purchased on Khao San Road. Dreads is straight Khao San. Mike doesn't really want to talk to Dreads anymore. What he wants to do is find Dorr. He wants to impress Analect, not Bishop. He wants to meet this man who boxed his father.

At 2 A.M. the strobes stop and the PA blares that it is time to leave. This is exactly Mike's story, backpacker kids and how the government is cracking down on the ecstasy scene, instituting a two o'clock closing time. People begin to filter out. Mike starts to go with them, but Dreads hands him another beer and tells him to relax. "No worries man, what'll they arrest us for?"

For being stupid, thinks Mike.

The PA fires again: "THE POLICE WILL BE HERE IN FIVE MINUTES . . ." and then it becomes garbled and everyone is leaving. Mike is tired but Dreads says he knows a place they can go to and tells Mike about an apartment, just a few blocks away. Dreads gets excited talking about how the apartment is like a secret society of cool backpackers where there is always good hash. "Plus," he explains, "there are always girls there, white girls, you know? Not that the Thai girls aren't totally cool."

Mike looks at Dreads and knows that he is afraid of Thai girls.

Dreads keeps talking about the apartment and the "rad old guy" whose place it is. "And you should see his hookup," says Dreads as they walk out, "an older chick with red hair, so hot."

Outside, Mike sees two monster sports cars, hundred-thousand-dollar, 4 million baht, candy-colored, speed machines. Their brown, hair-gelled drivers open the doors and white girls with blond hair and slender bodies get in. Mike hadn't seen them inside. Probably rich Indian or Bengali kids, on holiday. They are loud, speeding into the night.

The walk to the apartment is longer than Mike expects, and Dreads talks the whole way, bragging about drugs. As a kind of experiment, Mike tells him he is doing a story about kids coming to Bangkok just to get high.

"Cool," says Dreads. "You can write about me."

8

The day before he left for Hong Kong, Mike was worried. For a day and a half his parents had not been speaking to each other with such cruelty that Mike became apprehensive about their future and the future of his family. Worrying slowed him down, though, so he tried to think of better times.

He thought of his mother skiing in Sun Valley, Idaho. She blew great powdery swaths of snow into the air as she raced down the mountain in front of him. She skied beautifully. He saw men watch her, in her yellow snowsuit, as she flew past them, and he was proud of her. She encouraged her sons to go full speed down the slopes. Why turn? she liked to say.

Their father asked her privately if she was crazy. They'll get hurt, he said. They're already berserk. But she brushed him off and told the boys very theatrically to snowboard like young gods racing in the sky. Mike and Lyle were more or less invincible on the mountain, and they raced and slipped through the pines at full speed, and even invented an out-of-bounds run on the back side of the mountain that they jokingly called "young gods."

The next year their father was injured on an icy inter-mediate run early in the morning on the third day of their trip. Only Mike saw him go down, breaking his arm in the kind of surprising fall an athlete takes at fifty. After that, Mike never thought of himself as a young god racing in the sky but, rather, as just a person much younger than his father. Just very young. This happened to Mike a lot when he started remembering the times he'd had with his father as a kid.

9

Mike follows Dreads up a narrow staircase. The apartment is in a peeling building over an Internet café. Dreads knocks on the door and says his name. Locks shoot and click before the door swings open. There is a mountain of backpacks just inside the door, and Mike has to step around the framed, zippered burdens.

"Welcome," comes an Australian accent.

Several kids look up at Mike; they're all pierced and a little raggedy but too white and western to be really ragged. They sprawl on the floor or lounge on wooden benches along the walls, an audience. The Australian sits on a cushion in the middle of the room. He has frizzed, gray hair and wears a vest but no shirt, lots of chains. He looks twice as old as most of the kids and seems to Mike to weave like a snake charmer. He is holding a joint.

"Mike," says Dreads, sweeping his arm at the Australian, "this is the famous Hardy."

"So, what brings you to Bangkok and would you like a pull?" Hardy asks.

"I'm fine, thanks," Mike says.

"He's a reporter," says Dreads.

Stupid, thinks Mike, but he sees some of the kids get more interested.

"Well, not much going on around here," Hardy says, evenly, producing a lacy bra from under his cushion. He begins to play a kind of cat's cradle with it between his fingers, joint at his lips.

"For a travel magazine," Mike says. "Just a good vacation, really."

"I'm sure."

Mike nods. Hardy studies him and says, "Did you know there is a doctor in California who has a cure for cancer?"

Mike doesn't say anything and a girl in a pirate bandanna whom Hardy calls Lucy rises from the heap of kids at his feet and makes her way through a beaded curtain to the kitchen. Mike is careful not to stare at her long, tan legs rising up into her cutoff jeans.

"We only started getting cancer recently," Hardy continues. "It was you Americans, treating everything. But this stuff . . ." Lucy Long Legs is back with a bowl of noodles and a pair of chopsticks and sits down between Hardy's legs. ". . . this stuff is just about as organic as you can get."

Mike asks him how long he's been in Bangkok. Hardy wraps his legs around Lucy Long Legs and puts down his joint. She feeds him some noodles.

"He's been here going on fucking twenty-two years," Dreads says.

"Can't trust a single motherfucker in this whole town," Hardy says through a mouthful of noodles. "Never could."

Mike asks if Hardy can point him to a place where he might score some pills. For the travel story. Mike doesn't want the pills, he just wants to ask for them.

"No problem, somethin' like a couple pills," Hardy says, and resettles his crotch before continuing, "How about a girl, too? Local, the real Thai experience. I've got just the one."

"No thanks," Mike says, noticing that Hardy is slurring his words. How high is this guy? he wonders.

"Yeah, a girl can be trouble," Hardy goes on. "She has you because you want to fuck her, so she drugs you and pinches your schwee, or she is set up with a cop and they shake you down. Happened to me three or four times, but I been here going on twenty-two years now."

"Cops were coming to the club," Dreads volunteers. "That's why we left."

Hardy nods knowingly. "They lock the door and make everybody piss in a cup," he says. "It's not the same here, not like it was in the old days."

Mike looks at Hardy and thinks about how he never wants to have any *old days*. But "Yeah," he says. "I'm on the lookout for a friend of a friend who was here back then. His name is Christopher Dorr, American reporter guy. He's supposed to be living in Bangkok somewhere."

"Dorr, yes, can't say I know him personally, though." Hardy pulls on his joint again. "But I reckon I've heard of him. Then again," he exhales, "every other bugger you meet is looking for his contact, isn't he? A lot of stories out there."

"Far-out," says Dreads.

"Long-lost fellas who went to earth," Hardy says, smiling.

"Went to earth?" Mike asks.

"Like me," Hardy snorts. "Went to earth and now I eat fire." He sucks down to the end of the roach and then flicks it up in the air, smoking, and catches it in his mouth. The backpackers almost applaud. Hardy swallows.

Way over the top, thinks Mike. He looks at Hardy carefully and decides that he is very high, but not necessarily from the joint.

"There are, at any given time, some fifty righteous men on the planet," Hardy says. "These righteous don't know it, but if it weren't for them, God would blow the whole place to hell. And here's the catch, see: as soon as one finds out he's one of the chosen, he dies and somebody else, some other righteous soul, takes his place."

The sprawled backpackers are captivated. Lucy Long Legs is indulgent but interrupts. "Do you want to watch a movie?" She rises from Hardy's crotch and rummages in a cabinet.

A stir of approval from the backpackers and Hardy picks *Casablanca*. Mike leans against the wall, sometimes watching the movie on the little television in the corner, but mostly watching Lucy Long Legs as she nods out on Hardy's lap. Blond hair spills out from under her Jolly Roger bandanna and Mike sees a tattoo on her ankle. She looks very young.

10

Mike's father, Mike's mother, Elliot Analect, Dorr, and Dorr's twin sister were all students at Harvard when they met. The three boys were roommates but they shared more than an address. They all wanted to be writers and were very competitive, especially Mike's father and Dorr. As freshmen, all three became marginally famous for driving Dorr's beat-up 1953 Chevy convertible down the frozen Charles River, past the boathouse where the Radcliffe winter formal was taking place. The story was that they put down the top just as they came into view, just before the car broke through the ice—and therefore just in time to allow them to escape. This was not exactly true.

The Holworthy boys, as they came to be known, after Holworthy Hall, their freshman dorm, became very close during the four years. At the end, they were something like brothers.

Mike's father and Dorr often sparred in the late afternoon and then went for a drink or several afterward. Dorr was a great talker and a decent boxer. These fighting and drinking sessions were Mike's father's favorite times. Dorr had schemes, places to go, women to fuck. He was exuberant and frequently drunk, and Mike's father envied him for the way he didn't seem to think too much about anything. Spending time with Dorr turned Mike's father into a heavy smoker.

Analect was never as close with Mike's father and Dorr. He did not drink as much and did not box at all. Unlike them, Analect had grown up with both of his parents. He was a third-generation legacy at Harvard and, by the time he was eighteen, already very good at not fucking up, something that saved Dorr and Mike's father from expulsion on several occasions. Thinking about this, Analect decided it was a trade-off he was willing to accept: two real parents for two fake brothers.

11

The movies run late and the morning seeps through the shuttered windows. Mike says "Thanks for your hospitality" to an unconscious room as he picks his way through to the door.

As he opens it, a Thai man is opening it from the other side. Mike apologizes across the languages and brushes past him. The Thai man stands in the doorway and takes a small package wrapped with rubber bands from the pocket of his jeans and wings it at sleeping Hardy's forehead. The Thai man reacts with a high-pitched laugh and is following Mike down the stairs before Hardy registers the whack.

Down on the street, Mike wonders where to go for a cab. The Thai man walks quickly to a parked motorcycle, turns, and calls back to him.

"Taxi? Taxi! Cheap." He is wearing a blue vest with a number and an advertisement for a taxi service on it. His movements are quick and jerky as he gestures for Mike to get on behind him.

"How much?" Mike asks, as he approaches the bike.

"A hundred and twenty." The Thai man bounces up and down on his seat, gunning the engine.

How much is that? Mike wonders. Whatever. "Sure," he says, getting on the bike.

The driver offers him a helmet, which he declines, and they are off. Mike is glad for the handholds at his side so that he doesn't have to hold on to the driver. The motorcycle flies and weaves on the wide boulevards and sends the cloth of the produce stalls flapping as they shoot the alleys.

They join a wide line of bikes at the first light they don't make. Mike looks over to the next motorcycle and sees a Thai girl. She is wearing white sweatpants and a T-shirt, and long black hair hangs in a shimmer between her shoulder blades. Her complexion is dark and clear like tea. She has a bundle of something at her chest that Mike can't quite see.

The girl suddenly catches Mike looking at her and smiles a shy, sweet smile that surprises him and snaps his head back to looking straight ahead. The light changes and the girl speeds forward, hair blowing out behind her, leading the charge of the motorcycles into the morning. As Mike catches up he sees that she is holding a naked brown baby.

When Mike sees the baby he is distracted, so he doesn't see the crash coming.

The driver is gunning. Mike has never been on a bike like this before. It is much faster than he imagined. And then, just as the slow skid begins, Mike realizes what made him nervous about his driver. His eyes. The driver is high.

Mike tries to lean into the skid or away from it; he doesn't know, just tries to exert some force, change it. The bike is almost scraping his leg on the cement. Mike wants to turn it all down, like a radio. Horns bleat, cars veer out of the way. Mike's mind ricochets off the instant possibilities of hitting the car they just cut off or of being broadsided by another. He grits his teeth and holds on. This might be it, he thinks, for the first time in his life. It's a sickening realization, a deep and awful nausea that he feels, death maybe, flying underneath him. And then it all stops.

On the other side of the intersection, the driver looks around as if he has lost something. He is speaking to himself in Thai and all Mike can say to him, tapping him on the shoulder, is, "Khao San Road?"

They take off again, and looking down at his pant leg, Mike sees that it did scrape, and there is blood, running in smudges, down to his ankle.

Mike's hotel is either right here or down at the other end. He has the heady feeling of a wild night, danger that has passed. He can look anyone in the eye and tell them—I was out. I was doing something. I did not just stay in my room and watch TV the way I wanted to. I did not just cross the street and drink beer until I got sleepy. I did not just chat with backpackers or visit a temple a couple minutes from the hotel. I went out there. I talked with Hardy and saw Lucy Long Legs and almost died on a motorcycle. I went.

The hotel, it turns out, is right in front of him.

12

"Don't forget," Mike's father told him on the way to the airport, "Hong Kong is only eighteen hours away."

Mike drank a beer with his parents at an empty airport bar. His mother remarked that time always seemed to stand still for her in airports. "Time and space," she said, "are in the same continuum. This is not space," she went on, sweeping her arm over the plastic bar, "so there's no time."

Mike's father rolled his eyes. Mike laughed and sipped his beer, but he was thinking about all the planes his mother had missed. When she ordered shots of tequila, he said he wanted to go to the gate, even though he had plenty of time. He shook his father's hand and kissed his mother on the cheek and promised to be in touch. They told him not to worry about staying in touch. "We'll be OK," said his mother.

"Regards to Analect," said his father.

Mike walked away toward the gate. Looking over his shoulder, he could see his parents at the bar. They looked ridiculous, still not talking. The bartender placed two shot glasses in front of them, and Mike saw his mother pull one of the glasses to her lips and throw the shot down her throat. Her head jerked back like someone had punched her in the chin. He had never seen his mother drink a shot before, and in that instant he thought of all the drunk kids at school, sweating and red-faced, going shot for shot across dorm desks.

His mother looked at his father and at the shot still in front of him. He did not look at her. Then she took his shot and drank it in one long, slow sip, and Mike saw his mother call the bartender over again.

13

Mike wakes up as the sun is going down and looks at the evening sky, thick and red, out his window. He wants to wolf down the candy bars in the minifridge, but he knows this would show up on the magazine's bill and he doesn't want to look like he was just hanging around the hotel.

He goes to the café across the street and has an evening breakfast of rolls and noodles with a French paraglider girl who just walks over and sits down next to him.

"I'm leaving in a few days," she says.

"Where are you going?"

She is headed up north to Chiang Mai to go parasailing or hang gliding and to otherwise get high. They smoke cigarettes and drink coffee together.

"I know some good bars around here," she says.

Mike wants to go to one of her bars and tell her his story of last night. He is about to suggest they do this, go to a bar, when she says that Thailand has expanded her consciousness and brought her closer to God. Not really God, but the state of truly organic being. She can actually feel her aura expanding, right now.

Mike goes back to his room and writes this down in his notebook. He realizes Bangkok is probably full of these people.

There is no message for Mike on his cell, no message on his room phone. He wants to tell Bishop about his night with the backpackers and how, maybe, Hardy is the center of the story. But Bishop is not in his room. Mike knocks, waits for five minutes, and knocks again to be sure.

No surprise, thinks Mike, as he walks back down to the lobby. Bishop told him he'd be making up for lost time with his girl. Mike thinks she must be Thai. He imagines a woman putting on her best yellow dress and red lipstick and rushing in white high heels to meet Bishop at a bar he has gone straight to after dropping Mike off at the hotel. Maybe they know Bangkok very well and love it together, and take long walks through the winding streets that smell of peanut and sweet smoke. But Mike knows, from the way Bishop said "best girl," that this is not how it is. Mike hopes the woman in the yellow dress makes good money, whoever she is. This is what Mike is thinking as he crosses Khao San Road.

The road is crowded, always. It is crowded with *farangs*. It's famous for this. "A *farang*," Bishop told Mike, "is a Caucasian. Especially like you," he said.

Mike is not hungry, but for something to do he orders a bowl of noodles from a street vendor and watches the lady crack an egg into boiling water. Bishop had warned him about street noodles. "Sometimes they get you and sometimes they don't," he said. "It can take a couple days. But that's how Bangkok is, it sneaks up on you."

Behind the street vendor, the motorcycle taxi drivers are lounging, smoking, and looking at backpacker asses browsing the cheap hemp clothing. Next to the motorcycle taxis an old man sits at an easel, the way an old painter might sit along the East River in New York. He is making fake IDs. These are not driver's licenses—like the ones Mike's friends back home get so they can buy beer—but international student IDs, passports, and documents to get discounts or through borders in the north. Very poor fakes. As the woman hands over the egg noodles, Mike realizes that he should have checked at the desk for messages. He eats his food quickly and returns to the hotel.

The lobby is empty and Mike's shoes are loud on the hardwood floor. He asks the two pretty Thai girls behind the front desk if there are any messages for him.

"No, no, sorry."

"Are you sure?"

"No, no, sorry." The girls are about Mike's age and smiling at him unhelpfully. He knows they will chitter when he turns to go.

"How about for my friend Mr. Bishop?"

"Oh, but I am sorry, we cannot show other guest messages."

Mike knows what he has to do and smiles big but sad at the girls.

"But he's my boss, and I'm supposed to be arranging his meeting, and the people who sent the message didn't know my name."

The girls smile and laugh. This *farang* could be trouble. He's cute, though, and maybe a big tipper. They show him the fax that came in for Mr. Bishop.

The message reads: "Forty-four Bar @ Soi 4 Silom 9:00 you owe me. MB."

Mike imagines with dread trying to relay this address to whatever driver he recruits and wonders what is owed.

14

Mike's grandfather died in World War II, leaving Mike's father as the last scion of a San Francisco import-export family. The family thought Mike's grandmother was not quite up to standard, a charity case their lost son would have gotten over if he hadn't died on the beach at Iwo Jima. She raised Mike's father while warring with the family in their big house in Pacific Heights, and by the time Mike's father turned eighteen, he was glad to leave for college.

Mike's mother was from New York. She met Mike's father on the first day of college and everyone said they looked alike. Her father was a councilman whose roots in city politics could be traced back to Tammany Hall. She inherited the ability to talk to everybody like they were the only person in the room. She graduated at the top of her Stuyvesant class.

Dorr and his sister were the exotics. They grew up Catholic in New Orleans and were orphaned at age twelve. Their parents died in a fire, which Dorr said, when he said anything about it, was set by the ghosts of slaves. From then on, they lived with a widowed aunt. The siblings were very close but never incestuous. Trust funds paid for Harvard.

It was Analect's idea that the five of them have brunch every Sunday. The tradition started at the end of freshman year. His joke was that he liked to have his omelet with two eggs and two sets of twins. They all drank Bloody Marys. A lot of the things they wound up doing were Analect's idea.

15

Mike hopes Bishop will show up but knows he won't. He waits anyway, sitting across the street from the hotel at his café. He orders Coke after Coke. They come in tall, narrow glass bottles, different than in the U.S., and he tries to pace himself. As he watches for Bishop walking in or out of the hotel, he thinks about Christopher Dorr. Makes up stories, actually.

Maybe Dorr was a spy, had a cover as a journalist, but was actually working for the government, bugging hotel rooms, assassinating warlords, fucking cultural attachés. Shit like that. Or maybe he had become consumed by his own writing and couldn't be bothered with the journalism anymore, rising at dawn every day, punching at a steel typewriter on some overgrown roof garden. Why not? His piece on the Wa was beyond journalism. Or maybe Dorr had finally realized he was a woman and was right now at a club in Patpong in high-heeled boots and purple makeup. Whatever. Mike would find his body, hot with bullets, in a bloodied bathroom and have to go after the killers. Maybe he had married a wealthy dope-dealer widow and spent his days watching animated movies on thick carpeting with his young stepchildren—and the hell with Analect and all the rest of it. All bullshit for sure.

Analect had said that he and Dorr and Mike's father were like brothers once, but Mike's father had never talked about it. Mike thinks about this. Why didn't his father ever say anything? He had always spoken freely about Analect. Maybe there was an argument. Mike imagines the three of them drunk and arguing about nothing, like some of the popped-collar fools he goes to school with. The argument is so loud they can neither remember nor forgive it the next morning. The argument is about money or women or God or art or sports but really is about which of them is the best, because they all know that one of them is but they don't know who yet.

Maybe none of it is important. Maybe they weren't at all like brothers, and Analect just said they were. Or maybe brotherhood is completely gaseous, and theirs dissipated thirty years ago in the air behind jet planes and thrown wedding bouquets. Mike doesn't know.

It gets to be eight o'clock and Mike has called Bishop's cell phone and left another message, but there is still no sign of him. It is so hot, even in the breezy night, that Mike is sweating through his shirt. He knows that he will have to go to the bar by himself.

A "soi" is a road Mike thinks he remembers, but he has no sense of distance yet in Bangkok. The motorcycle taxis are right there, handy. But maybe he should walk and find a cab at the end of the road. No, he decides, what are the chances of two motorcycle skids? He approaches the pack of lounging drivers and shows one of them the address. As the driver makes a display of looking at it, Mike realizes he cannot read.

"Soi Four, Silom," says Mike, and the driver nods vigorously. Mike looks into his eyes for maybe a moment too long, weirds the guy out a little, but he has to be sure.

And then the wonder of a clean motorcycle ride through Bangkok. Mike leans into the turns, watches the city slide past him. Wild dogs everywhere and carts of rice and vegetables. In one neighborhood, bald men in red robes. Buddhists, but out at night? Maybe Dorr has become a monk, solitary even among the red robes, and is marching home from prayer to sleep on a yellowing woven mat. Mike wishes he could stay on the motorcycle all night and all day, never have to talk to anyone, just soak it all in at high speed. If he could only see it all in motion, he thinks, he could have the insight without the fear, the trip without the nerves.

The story without the work. Mike wonders if Analect knew this would happen.

Mike gets to Silom Road in twenty minutes. It's only eight-thirty and he doesn't want to be early. Then, swinging his leg over the back of the motorbike, he hears a rip.

"Ha." The driver points at Mike's ripped pant leg as Mike pays him. Mike nods and laughs, but he is thinking Goddamn it, because he has ripped his expensive New York no-pleat safari pants right up the inseam. His father got him those pants.

Mike looks up and down Silom Road, sees Soi Four and walks down the smaller street looking for any numbered building. Where is 44? He can't find it, but then, at a dead end, a sign that reads .44 Bar. The .44 Bar. Like a gun. Good.

To kill time, Mike walks back to Silom Road looking for new pants in the stalls that line the sidewalk. It is hard to walk in the crowd. He is not really looking for pants. He is looking for the version of himself that does not arrive too early.

He goes from stall to stall and all the pants are either a bad color or a bad cut or stop above the ankle, fisherman's pants. Hemp. A woman catches his eye and points to a bunch of metal rings on a string. They have designs painted on them, like the rings Dreads had on his thumb. Maybe no one will notice his pants.

Mike decides he wants a beer and to hell with not wanting to arrive too early in ripped pants.

16

The first real conversation Mike could remember having with his mother was about ambition. Before, there was only the buzz of childhood, and this conversation remained with him like a kind of demarcation. Mike was in sixth grade and had failed a test in Latin that day and he had never failed before. He cried in private before dinner, in hot frustration, and his mother caught him and decided to take him out—on an expedition, she called it—to calm him down, so that he wouldn't beat himself up the way Lyle always did. Lyle made himself sick, she said, doing schoolwork. Mike's mother was determined that her second son be more comfortable.

"Can't let the same thing happen twice," she said to Mike's father.

"Don't think too much," Mike's father said over his shoulder, loading the dishwasher. This pissed her off and she slammed the door. He finished the dishes because the maid was off the next day, and then looked in on Lyle, who was hunched over his trigonometry like a hawk protecting carrion.

*   *   *

Mike and his mother sat listening to a street jazz quartet in the plaza at the World Trade Center. Mike's mother said the weather, which was clear, made her want to fly up and see her floating reflection in the high windows as she listened to the hard bop. She hated to fly but now she said she wanted to.

This didn't cheer Mike up. He was still frowning. So his mother described to him how everybody failed sometimes. She pointed to the musicians.

"That's all improvisation is," she said, "a series of exchanged failures. No one ever gets it right. You think you get one thing, but then you find out you missed something else. You think you studied enough, but then you find out you haven't."

"Lyle never failed a test." Mike was still very frustrated. "Did you? Did Dad?"

"Your father's not always right," she said without meaning to. "Neither is Lyle," she added quickly. But Mike heard what she had said first, and that was part of the demarcation.

"I don't know why, Mike, but most people, most of the time, fail. Nobody gets what he or she wants. Everyone thinks they will in the beginning but then they don't. Usually they don't have enough money, so they aren't free. Sometimes they have the money but it doesn't matter because they aren't as successful as they should be. Or *think* they should be." Mike's mother went on and on until Mike realized that she wasn't talking about him and his test; she was talking about something else entirely. Mike interrupted her.

"*O di immortales! In qua urbe vivimmus? Quam civitatem habemus?*" he said.

"What?"

"It was on my test today. It's the only thing I got right."

"What does it mean?"

"O immortal gods! In what city do we live? What society do we have?"

She looked at her son frowning on the bench next to her and began to cry.

"I'm OK about the test," Mike said, "really, it's OK."

"I know, Mike," she said, and pulled herself together. "I was just so proud of you, just now."

Mike knew that wasn't why she cried.

17

The .44 Bar is an English-speaking pub, paneled in dark wood, with a football match droning on the one television. Mike goes to the bar and orders a beer. He wants to order right, in case anybody's watching. Nobody cares, he reminds himself, scanning the scattered groups of expats. Nobody looks like an "MB," no lone journalist waiting for Bishop at the bar.

However, in a booth near the pool table Mike notices a redheaded woman and a blond man with his hair topknotted like a samurai. They are laughing about something and watching a small but very tough-looking black guy with a shaved head handily beat a very much larger man at nine-ball. Mike remembers the hookup that Dreads told him about, the redhead, but then lets it go when he remembers something Bishop told him about everyone in Bangkok looking like a dope dealer if you're looking for one.

Mike edges down the bar and hears something from the redhead about tiger teeth, smuggled aphrodisiacs in a false-bottomed boat. Mike can tell that the redhead is pissed off about something and decides that, whoever she is, he would never want to cross her. Then suddenly she laughs again. Her anger was just part of the way she was telling the story. The guy in the topknot gesticulates like a conductor as he starts talking, something about a particular cop and the gusto with which he is celebrating the birth of his first son. He is the cop to go to these days because he is in such fine spirits.

Mike wishes Bishop would show up. He orders another beer and moves closer to the booth to hear better. The topknot guy pulls up his legs and sits cross-legged and straight-backed with a new story. "So the soldiers walk us in and take off the blindfolds and the general is standing on one side of a little glass coffee table and he's tiny, like this, full uniform, the whole thing, dress for the camera, and Harrison . . ."

The bald guy playing pool, Harrison apparently, nods to confirm the story.

". . . Harrison has got that fat motor drive of his with the 85x150 zoom hanging over his shoulder. And as he reaches out to shake hands with the general the strap slips somehow . . ."

Harrison wears a small, tight grin and sips his drink.

". . . and the camera crashes down on top of this glass table-top and shatters right through. So we freeze and every guy in the room has his gun pointed at us . . ." Topknot imitates the sound of a gun cocking. It's remarkably realistic.

". . . everyone is dead silent for a second, and then the little general, he just goes, 'hahahaha,' and all the rest of them start laughing too, 'hahaha.' And we're looking at each other, laughing our bloody arses off, 'hahaha,' and then we all sit down and have beers."

Mike is thinking how it all sounds like something out of a

comic book when a strong finger taps him from behind, not on his shoulder but exactly on the tip of a vertebra. Mike spins.

It's the leathery bald guy, Harrison. "Do I know you?" he asks.

Mike knows instantly that Harrison has caught him eavesdropping. His heart thuds in his chest and he concentrates on speaking slowly. He introduces himself and explains that he is looking for a reporter with the initials *MB*. The topknot guy laughs behind him.

Mike turns again and feels his face warming, the last thing he wants, and now the redhead is staring at him, too, and he knows he is blushing.

"Mickey Burton," Topknot says, "at your service." He sticks out a hand from his cross-legged seat and cocks his head at Mike. "I was expecting Tommy Bishop."

"I'm his assistant."

"Really?" Burton asks. "Hilarious. You better sit down and have a drink. Welcome to the flying circus."

18

There, sitting around the table, Burton formally introduces Mike to the redhead, Bridget, and the giant, Paul, and again to Harrison. They are all freelance but not broke. Burton rattles off résumés that sound to Mike right out of Kipling, except these are set in East Timor or involve going into the jungle with the death squads or, most recently for Burton, watching a Buddhist temple blow up in southern Thailand—"idol arms flying through the air."

Burton goes on and on. Bridget is from Sydney and is working on a photo book about endangered animals, how they are poached and smuggled all over Southeast Asia and Africa. Paul recently returned from chasing pirates across the South China Sea and is working on his own book about how modern piracy is a billion-dollar industry. Burton is hypnotic, practiced, and self-deprecating as he describes their exploits, but when he gets to Harrison's story, Harrison stops him and redirects the talk to Mike.

"What's your story?" he asks, and Mike is surprised by how interested they all seem. They pay close attention as he explains how Analect sent him with Bishop. It's as if he were just as compelling as guns in the jungle. It's kind, Mike thinks, but it's also spooky.

"I get it," Burton says. "Shrewd, shrewd Analect. You can pass for one, so you set up a bunch of backpackers for Bishop. A bit of a travel piece. And you're his decoy."

That last word surprises Mike. Paul sits down heavily next to him and leans in. "Sounds like a bullshit story," he says, in an Eastern European accent Mike can't place.

"Ecstasy's not so bad a story, you see." Burton laughs, as if translating. "But it's a bit of an easy thing to come in here looking for, and Paul's a bit perturbed on account of your focus on that, given the other pill story."

"*Yaa baa.*" Mike wants them to know he knows something, that he did his homework.

"But do you know about the silence killings?" Burton asks. "That's what's been happening in Thailand. Hundreds here, maybe more up north."

"Toxic Thaksin," adds Bridget.

Mike knows that Thaksin Shinawatra is the prime minister of Thailand.

"Did your man Bishop tell you what he was up to tonight?" asks Burton.

"No, I haven't spoken to him since we got to the hotel."

"Have you checked in with Hong Kong? Analect would probably like to hear from you." Burton fingers his topknot with a tan, veined hand. "What did he say to you, actually?"

Mike tells them that Analect also told him to look up Christopher Dorr. This produces looks of surprise between Bridget and Burton that they quickly gloss over. But Mike notices, and is glad he did not tell them Dorr was a friend of his father.

"Let's have another round and think about this," says Burton, and goes to the bar. Bridget is staring at Mike again. He smiles and looks down at his empty bottle.

"So what are you planning on doing, Mr. Mike?" Bridget's voice is low and even.

"Well, I'm not sure," he says, feeling himself blush again. "I suppose I'll keep working on the story myself and wait to hear from Bishop. It's really just asking backpacker kids questions."

"It always turns more complicated than you think," she says, looking at Mike over the forest of bottles on the table.

Mike knows this already.

19

Mike's parents' house on Long Island was constructed of old beams, and the cedar shingles were gray and weathered by nearness to the sea. The living room smelled of dry wood and salty air, and also candles. Mike's mother adored expensive candles, and she burned them constantly, especially over the winters, which was strange for a woman who claimed to be so afraid of fire. She said the house would go up like a box of matches if they weren't all very careful.

One winter night, the living room fireplace spat an ember onto one of their mother's small Persian carpets. She had been alone in there all evening. The boys had eaten with their father and he had already tucked them into bed. He was in the kitchen making a drink when he heard his wife scream. The boys ran to the stairs a moment later and saw their father spraying the rug with a yellow fire extinguisher. The gray exhaust overwhelmed the whole room and seemed overcompensation for the circle of black ash burned in the rug. Mike's mother was sobbing and yelling at her husband. He sprayed the rug a last time, sprayed the fireplace, and then put down the extinguisher and looked at her.

She screamed, how could he not have noticed? Was he drunk? Did he maybe even want the house to burn down, so that he could start again somewhere else? None of this made sense to Mike and Lyle, but they didn't forget it. Their mother was in only her robe, and it kept slipping open. She didn't seem to care. And somehow her nakedness, combined with her yelling, paralyzed the boys on the staircase. It took their father a few moments to register their presence and then shepherd them back up to bed. Turned out she was drunk.

20

"Come with us, will you?" asks Burton, almost too politely. "You really ought to. We're going to my place. I've also got just the thing, a good contact for you, a police lieutenant. I'll write down his number."

"Maybe I should leave a note for Bishop," says Mike.

"I wouldn't worry about him," says Burton. "In fact, I'd forget about him."

Mike feels like he's been adopted, or at least let in on some kind of private joke. And no one has said anything about the rip in his pants.

"Thaksin wants every drug dealer in the country dead," says Bridget. "Come with us and we'll tell you about it. You don't want to write a backpacker story."

"You'll see," says Paul. "Cops on dealers, dealers on dealers." But Mike can see in Paul's dilated eyes that he's not sure about the invitation. "I'll meet you there," Paul continues. "I have to make a stop."

Mike notices, following Paul out the door, how heavy and high his shoulders are, how big his fists—how enormous the man actually is, like a bouncer headed for work, going into the neon lights of the Silom district.

It's strange, suddenly piling into a car with these new people, driving off with them through the warm rain in the Bangkok night. Mike admires the way Burton directs the driver. The rain splashes and crystallizes the light through the windows of the damp cab. No one speaks. Mike is in the backseat between Harrison and Bridget. She looks out the side window, and Burton and Harrison stare straight ahead; they are all quiet for a moment. Harrison strokes his bald head and closes his eyes. Mike is acutely aware of the point at which his leg leans up against Bridget. She smells of sweet pepper. Mike is keyed up and a little drunk and feels good. He says something like thanks for taking me around, then feels it was premature for thanks.

"Oh please," says Burton.

Bridget nods, though she is still looking out the window.

21

Mike's father, Dorr, and Analect were all in love with Mike's mother, but it was his father who had her first. Neither of them had been in love before. They had sex everywhere, including the library. The affair was even fiercer because of the tension between Mike's mother and Dorr. Analect saw what would happen a long way off.

Over Thanksgiving break their senior year, Mike's father found out that she was cheating on him with Dorr. Boston was three hours into the first snow of the year. Mike's father had the cab turn around halfway to Logan when he heard on the radio that all flights were grounded because of the storm. He had been dreading San Francisco anyway. He returned to Lowell House and there they were, drunk in bed together. No one knew what to do.

Mike's father found Analect in a bar on Mass. Ave. Analect pretended to be surprised and lied that he didn't know anything about it.

By the time the snow stopped falling, Mike's father had slept with Dorr's sister as revenge.

22

A refuge from the wild traffic, up a road in some corner of the city. Gardens and houses, no carts on the side of the road. Getting out of the cab, Mike sees an elephant fountain spraying water from its trunk. Burton's apartment is behind the elephant in a compound originally occupied by French soldiers. Up the wide stone stairs, five flights of them, Burton's door is painted blue.

The apartment isn't huge but it has two long couches, a television, a bar, books. One wall is covered in hanging two-foot lengths of yellowed rope. A terrace and a hot tub. Burton pours drinks for everybody and the four of them simultaneously light cigarettes.

Mike asks about the rope, testing the feel of it against his knuckles.

"Conceptual decor," says Burton.

"Those are all from boxing matches along the Burmese border," says Harrison. "They wrap the rope around their hands."

Mike knew that already, but he isn't sure how.

Paul arrives shortly, carrying clinking bodega bags of green-bottled beer. He walks in talking, as if to announce himself with some kind of monologue. Mike feels like he's heard it all before, even though he hasn't. "The problem in Thailand," says Paul, "is not *farangs*. Yes, *farangs* are annoying. They visit just to fuck the women. Some maybe go to earth and stay, OK. I'm a *farang*." Mike wonders if anyone besides him is listening. "But the real problem," says Paul, "is Thais who want to be *farangs*. Bananas. Yellow on the outside, white on the inside. They fuck up the system. They say they're cleaning it up but they are the dirtiest."

Mike sees that Paul is particularly upset by the notion of dirty.

Mike sits in an easy chair watching Burton chop white pills into halves. Paul eats a whole one and Burton eats a half. Mike is surprised by the lack of ceremony, especially compared to the way he's seen every stoner back home get high—so very, very carefully.

"Have you ever taken ecstasy?" Paul asks.

"No," says Mike.

"Man, watch out," Paul says. He sighs and suddenly seems very tired. Mike realizes Paul is either drunk or high, probably both. "The fucking cops are everywhere," he says, "but don't worry, it's always too early for dread."

Mike has no idea.

Burton looks at him. "Would you like a pill, Mike?"

Mike shakes his head. Not now, he thinks. Sometime, maybe soon, but not now.

Burton has changed into a loose shirt and great baggy silk pants. He sits on a footstool next to Mike's chair. His blond hair is now let down from the topknot and loose about his eyes.

"I tend not to do hard drugs."

"You've tried some, then?"

Mike smoked weed occasionally back home. It made him stupid and slightly sleepy and he usually did it with Jane and they would fuck and watch a movie.

"Yeah, I had a bad time recently."

"What happened?" Burton asks, and Mike is not surprised, somehow, by how easily the lies come.

"I'd been smoking and drinking with my girlfriend and some people at a party on the roof of this building, and I think there must have been some weird shit in the weed, because it made me sort of nuts."

"That's no good," Burton says, tapping down a cigarette.

"I know," continues Mike, "made me want to jump off the roof." He says this half solemn and half not, like someone, he thinks, who is too cool to brag about nearly tossing himself off the roof but who is too honest to lie about it. Burton seems to be taking him at his word. They all are. Of course they are, Mike thinks. Why wouldn't they?

"Well, we won't let you jump off the roof."

They all talk to Mike about why he should do ecstasy. Why, Mike wonders. But they are very civil about it. Ecstasy is not like weed that will make you jump off the roof. It's friendlier. And we're all here. Couldn't be a safer place.

Mike thinks that, beneath it all, they are asking him a question. But what? And then suddenly he thinks of the girl on the motorcycle carrying the baby. Maybe he's high already.

The pill feels chalky for a moment on Mike's tongue and then he swallows.

23

As soon as Mike decided to take the internship in Hong Kong, his mother gave him a picture of the family. In it, Mike, his parents, and Lyle stand at the seashore near the house on Long Island. They look like catalog people, handsome and expensive, posed and shot.

Lying in bed a week before he was to leave, Mike held up the photograph to a lamp. He was wondering what his life would be like in Asia. The lamplight shone through the silver gelatin print, and Mike could see through himself. He could see through his blond hair and white teeth. He could see through his parents with their arms around each other, and his frowning brother. He could see through the sky behind his family and the sand they stood on.

Mike was determined that his life in Asia be good and simple. That it be the start of his life, Mike's life, and not be a crazy life. But as he looked at what was actually just a snapshot and saw his family ghosted by the backlight, he suddenly understood something new and it unsettled him. What Mike saw was the potential for craziness in himself, just like it was there in all of them.

24

Mike is high. He looks around the room and is struck, in the self-conscious and lengthy realizations of his synapses, by how ordinary everything is. Mike is beginning to suspect that he is himself as much a cliché as his new reporter friends. But he feels good. He thinks of the girl on the motorcycle with the baby and what she would say if she could open his head with a crowbar and read his thoughts, which roll around like so many ball bearings in there. Maybe she would ask him to marry her. Maybe she would rob him. Both appeal to Mike.

"Do you know an Australian named Hardy?" Mike asks Burton. It's like he can't help himself.

"Total stoner lech," says Burton, beginning yet another monologue. "His father was a lawyer but he grew up poor in Sydney because his father was obsessed with the Aboriginal women, wanted to fuck every single one he saw, and so his practice was dedicated to Aboriginal land preservation and he never made any money. Father and son started smoking hash together when he was twelve, which could have been good or bad depending on how you look at lawyers, because young Hardy was himself considering the law until his father was murdered and ritualistically mutilated in the outback by a cuckolded Abo. Poor Hardy, in rage and grief, left his beloved Australia and, not surprisingly, was broke upon arrival in Bangkok. But Bangkok being what it was then, he was able on that first afternoon to get fed, laid, and housed. Good place, he thought, so he stuck around, moved a little dope, just enough to get by. Life was easy and hazy, and mostly he fucked backpackers, boys and girls, because, as he saw it, somebody had to. Now it's twenty years later and he keeps a crash pad to fuck the backpackers. Been in love with Bridget for years."

"How do they know each other?"

"Everybody knows everybody here and I think I fancy a soak," Burton says. "Have you thought about the hot tub? It's quite lovely. And there's the quite lovely Bridget sitting in it."

Mike follows Burton's gaze to the terrace, where Bridget and Paul are waving to them from the tub.

Mike strips out of his ripped pants to his shorts at the edge of the hot tub. The tub is deceptively large and deep, with submerged benches.

"Will you look at that, Paul?" says Bridget. "Look at Mike."

Paul looks at Mike and Mike looks down at his own chest, his hand absently scratching.

"He's in such form!" says Bridget. "Look at his stomach."

Mike goes red in the face as he lowers himself into the water. So ordinary, it's like he's at home. He remembers blushing in other hot tubs. It's the drugs, Mike suddenly thinks. What kind of asshole feels fucked with because he's in good shape?

"I bet you were an athlete," Bridget tells him. He says he was, just stopped playing when he got to college. Could have played.

"Were you that good?" she asks him.

"Fastest white kid in the city," Mike hears himself say, then feels very stupid, very young.

"How old are you, Mr. Mike?"

"Nineteen."

"Oh, I knew it." Bridget brings her hand up to her mouth, teasing him. "You're just a baby!"

Mike wants to tell her he likes the world probably as much as she does. Paul, staring up into the night sky with his wide, pale arms stretched out along the edge of the tub, tells him he has a rip in his trousers. So they noticed, thinks Mike. Of course they noticed.

Burton calls from the kitchen for Mike to come and help with drinks. Mike steps out of the tub with the certainty of Bridget's eyes upon him. If only she had to get out of the tub before me, he thinks.

Mike likes making drinks with Burton in the kitchen. He looks at the newspapers on the bar as Burton breaks ice with a small steel mallet. Mike reads about world leaders embroiled in war and torture. The Republican candidate for president of the United States is a deeply religious man and is quoted as saying that God is on his side. This is not cool with Burton, who, tapping the paper with an angry finger and shaking his head, breaks off to go piss.

Mike picks up the mallet to test it and it feels good in his hand. He lights another cigarette and reads the bookshelf behind the bar. Some books he doesn't recognize about Southeast Asia and drug smuggling, and high fashion, and a couple he knows from his first-year philosophy course, St. Augustine, Kierkegaard.

Suddenly, Bridget's voice, sticky and harsh, comes from the terrace. She is swearing and calling for help. Mike looks and sees her straining in the tub, sees her body and her freckled breasts roll up over the top and her red hair falling in her eyes, and then she braces her knees and drives her hips forward, calling for help, pulling, afraid.

"Burton," she is yelling, "come on, you idiot."

Mike runs and sees that she is trying to pull Paul from the bottom, where he is sitting cross-legged, like a submerged Buddha. His hair floats like a pale lily pad just beneath the surface. Harrison and Burton both rush up behind Mike and together they haul the enormous Paul from the tub. He splutters and hacks, eyes closed as they get him onto a chair on the terrace. Mike noticed earlier that the chair's back is made of wrought iron angels. Paul is still coughing as he opens his eyes.

"I didn't realize he had been down there so long," says Bridget, calm now. "I was looking off the other way and then I looked and realized he was there at the bottom."

Paul's long, pale face has a blue cast and his eyes stare out into nothing. Burton leans down into his face, patting it gently and then less gently.

After another minute or two, Paul seems to focus on Burton.

"What happened," asks Burton. "What happened, Paul?"

"It felt so good, I didn't want to be coming up."

This sounds very spacey to Mike, as if through an airlock.

"It felt like being in chocolate mousse."

Harrison walks back into the living room and starts reading the paper.

25

Mike remembers the time Lyle burned himself with a bottle rocket. They were at the beach with their parents and a friend of Lyle's who was visiting for the weekend. The sand was cool on their feet and the June sky was cloudless. They had a small bonfire, and were sitting on blankets watching as Mike's father roasted yellow bell peppers and hot dogs on metal skewers for lunch.

The friend was describing his father to Mike and Lyle, and their parents were listening even as they had their own conversation, which is something they learned to do as parents. Mike and Lyle learned to do the same thing as children. The friend was joking about his father, a television writer, describing him as an artist shamed and oppressed by the wealthy financiers who worked in the same Midtown tower where he had his office. Mike and Lyle were both nodding and laughing at the notion. Then their mother interrupted them and said to the friend, "That's called a fish-out-of-water setup, and I believe any number of very successful sitcom writers keep offices in Midtown."

"No, I guess you're right," said the friend. "I know."

They finished eating in silence and looked out at the ocean. Then Mike's father told the boys to go look in the trunk of the car. There was something for them in there. At a newsstand in Chinatown he had bought a coffee can full of bottle rockets. Mike and Lyle and the friend ran to the trunk and then down to the water to set some of them off. Lyle was especially jumpy because his parents were arguing over the fire behind them. The bottle rockets punctuated their argument with short, screaming hisses and weak pops.

Mike remembered that one went off in Lyle's hand. He couldn't tell how it happened, because Lyle was being so careful. But it looked like Lyle held it too long, like he wanted to see what would happen. The rocket shot up like a cartoon insect trying to burrow into the bottom of Lyle's chin. And then it exploded. The bottom of Lyle's face turned black and swelled immediately. Their father ran down to the water and grabbed his son, stroking his hair as he looked at the burn. He picked up Lyle and carried him to the car. "I'm taking him to the hospital, stay with Mike," he said to his wife.

Lyle, through the pain, was glad to be with just his father in the car. It was better to be with just one parent than two. Mike, with his mother, was thinking the same thing. "Divide and conquer" was their joke several years later.

Years later, Mike and Lyle would be drinking in the co-op of that same friend, and the friend would be telling the bottle rocket story, and Mike would say quietly, he thought, to his brother, "You set that thing off into your chin."

"Hey, yeah," the friend said, "I always remembered it like you were trying to fucking blow your chin off."

"I'm just bullshitting with my brother," said Mike.

The friend thought, not for the first time, that the whole family was crazy.

26

The night is over. The first color of the day is rising into the sky. Mike is tired and sweated out and a little high still, and he is sitting outside with Burton. Bridget has gone into the bedroom and closed the door. Paul has fallen asleep inside, watching television. Harrison walked into the bathroom a few minutes earlier and Mike hears the shower raining behind the door.

Mike lights one last cigarette and looks out at the coming morning, much clearer up here than the day before on the street. He wants to keep talking to Burton but doesn't know what to say, other than to ask some lame question about credentials.

"What?" Burton asks, with one eye open through the veil of blond hair. His head is nodding and weaving.

"Don't I need credentials or something like that to talk to that cop you mentioned?"

Burton blows his hair out of his face and trains his one open eye on Mike. "Mike," he sighs, very tired, "don't worry about the cops."

Burton nods out, and Mike is thinking about how exhausted he is too when Harrison appears on the terrace beside him. He is freshly scrubbed and doesn't look tired at all.

"How about we go out," he says. "I'm hungry. You hungry? Eat off the booze. Breakfast beer. Introduce you to the Grace."

Burton is completely passed out now but Mike says thank you to him anyway.

27

The Grace Hotel is an air-conditioned tower with a bar in the basement that never closes. It's famous for this. The bar's walls and ceiling are blue and yellow tile and the light is soft but fluorescent. The floor is not sticky and the bartenders are jaded Thais wearing hotel badges. It is impossible to tell when the sun rises because there are no windows. All very obvious. There is also a bowling alley.

"I hate this place," says Harrison.

Then why are we here? Mike wonders, as they step out of the way of a tiny Thai girl and a Brit in an orange, tie-dyed shirt. The girl trips as she passes and Mike sees a small, brown breast pop out of her dress. As Harrison leads him to the bar Mike notices a group of prostitutes in one corner who are taller and whiter than almost everybody else in the room. Mike thinks they look Russian, although he knows no Russians. A couple of them have red hair, he notices.

"Not for your story," says Harrison, as he orders beers, "but interesting."

Mike decides the prettiest girl in the place is a tall Thai, who does little talking but lots of hair mussing. She wears jeans and a white blouse cut in a deep V. She has three drinks from three different men in front of her and is sipping from each of them. Unlucky that she has ended up at the Grace this late, Harrison explains. She has to make up time.

Mike goes to the bathroom and when he returns Harrison is talking to a Thai girl whose back is to Mike. She is small, wearing a silver, almost metallic dress that stops just above her knees. From the back she looks the way the girls Mike grew up with did when they were twelve or thirteen and trying to look older. Her hips are so narrow. But when she turns, he is startled by the heavy makeup and the way she stares at him. Mike thinks she is probably his age.

Harrison calls her Tweety.

"Always flitting in and out of trouble," Harrison says, smiling at her.

Mike extends his hand and Tweety takes it in both of hers and leans forward and kisses him on the cheek, saying something to Harrison in Thai. He says something back to her and Mike is surprised to hear the sharp language come so easily out of Harrison's wide mouth.

"Harrison," Tweety says in a high voice, "you have very handsome friend."

Harrison grunts and sips his beer. "Mike is doing a story on pills," he says.

"A reporter?" Tweety says. "But you look so young."

"I'm barely doing it." Mike can see the bags under her eyes.

Harrison explains that Tweety is a very good translator. Tweety nods at the praise. "Maybe I could translate for you," she says and puts her hand on Mike's arm.

Mike tells her that the club kids all speak English.

"Many stories," is all she says.

"Better stories," Harrison says, seriously. "Tweety lives in Khlong Toei. That's one of the neighborhoods where Thaksin is cracking down. You've seen a lot of pills, haven't you, Tweety?"

Tweety's expression hardens. "I have seen," she says.

Mike realizes Harrison is trying to help him and that they are talking about *yaa baa*, not ecstasy.

"What do you think?" asks Mike. "The government is too rough?"

"Many stories," she says, again.

When Mike asks Tweety if she has heard of Christopher Dorr, she is startled and looks at Harrison, whose expression doesn't change. Mike himself is a little nervous about his question and watches Harrison for a sign. Nothing. Finally, Tweety says yes, she knows Dorr. He is a reporter, but she has not seen him in a long time. She looks past Mike at an expat in a pinstripe suit just down the bar.

"Another *farang* asshole," Tweety says. She now seems a little drunk. Mike asks her again about Thaksin and his crackdown.

"Even this place, the Grace, was raided, " she says, loudly. "They made everyone pee in cup. Many are careful about coming now, too high."

The expat in the suit overhears this and is unsettled. "What's that?" he wants to know. "You say they'd make me piss in a cup?"

Tweety smiles at Harrison, who nods down the bar.

"Really, they make you piss in a cup?" the man asks again. Then he comes out with it, of course. "I had a tab of E last night."

Harrison shrugs to show that this is nobody else's problem, and the man pays up quickly and leaves. Of course Tweety meant for him to hear.

After another drink, Mike asks Tweety if she could help him meet Christopher Dorr.

"No, I do not see him anymore," she says. "But maybe I translate for you."

"Finding Dorr is where I could use some help," says Mike.

"It is not a good story," says Tweety.

28

Mike's girlfriend, Jane, was a very good student and also good at sex, a combination that Mike's father once told him was not unusual. She was studying classics and was a fine translator. Sometimes she quoted the *Iliad* to Mike in bed, in Greek. They had never had an argument. One time Mike asked her if she thought that was strange.

"Why would we argue?" she said. "We never do anything wrong to each other and we're rich white kids at fancy schools." Mike found that answer very unsatisfying but didn't tell her.

Before Mike left for Hong Kong, he and Jane had re-affirmed that they would remain faithful to each other. Jane was going to Greece for the summer, and they had a loose plan to meet up somewhere in Europe in early September before they went back to school. They would race to bed and then linger in cafés and talk about their adventures. They were both a little sad because they knew they would potentially meet lovers on their travels. But they were also both slightly nervous and so were glad to have each other as anchors. Or something.

Mike and Jane did not like talking about their relationship. Many of the people they knew at college liked discussing and dissecting romances. Mike and Jane weren't interested, and this was part of why they had been together since those Fridays in high school when they talked all night about their families. The other part, of course, was that both sets of parents were crazy. Mike told Jane that life with his parents was like bad weather that came and went, and she told him about her father cheating on her mother and her mother taking him back, time after time. Later, it would occur to both of them that they had been so concerned with their families that they really hadn't thought much about each other, and they would regret this. By then, though, it wouldn't matter.

29

When they leave the Grace, the sun is all the way up and the heat burns down. Harrison takes Mike to a restaurant that is a single room off an alley. It is tiled and cool, with a stove and sink and refrigerator and two tables. They sit with beers and Harrison tells the man at the stove what food they want. Rolls come, along with cold noodles and fried vegetables spiced in egg. Mike realizes he is eating too quickly. And that he wants to know more about Tweety.

"Tweety seems like an interesting hooker," he says, with instant regret.

Harrison does not seem to notice, just eats his noodles. "She likes journalists," he says finally. "Wants to be a writer."

"Can that happen?"

"You never know," says Harrison.

"She's really a hooker?"

"She does a lot of things, works as a translator and a fixer sometimes."

"You use her?" Mike asks.

Harrison trains his eyes on Mike. "We helped her get started doing it way back," he says. "It's not really that unusual and she's quite good. Burton and I have this story going that Tweety's helping with right now, actually. Her brother runs pills on his bike. She's introducing us to him and he's supposed to connect us to a factory. Good pictures, maybe."

"She didn't seem to like Christopher Dorr," Mike says.

"Do you know why Analect asked you and Bishop to find him?"

Mike shakes his head. "Bishop said he disappeared."

"Not exactly." Harrison lights a cigarette and shoots his eyes at Mike again. "Analect burned him on a source that year on the Wa story. Some people died."

"That's why he disappeared?"

"You'd have to ask him yourself."

"I'd like to."

"You've got your own reasons."

"I read the work."

Harrison chuckles at this and inhales hard on his cigarette, as if an important decision has been made, and then relaxes. Relaxes for the first time since they met seventeen hours ago, it seems to Mike. Not a lot, just that his shoulders ease a little.

"Fair enough," says Harrison. "I can introduce you if you want."

"Thank you," Mike says. "That would be great."

How does this work, Mike wonders. What will I owe him?

30

Mike wakes up, still a little buzzed, as the sun is going down. He slept on top of his bed again. He showers and then empties his pockets. In one pocket he finds the number of the police contact Burton gave him. He should call right away, but he doesn't want to pick up the phone. He doesn't know why but he's not ready. After a meal, he thinks.

He takes care dressing, much more than he does at home. What a joke, he thinks, a new expat anticipating the worldly glamour of foreign sidewalks where no one is looking. He can dress like a movie star. He leaves his clean, light shirt open an extra button, revealing the undershirt beneath. He does not shave. He combs his hair back and rolls up his sleeves. A clean, broad white guy in good clothing. I am not an easy mark, he thinks. He hopes.

Downstairs, Mike leaves another message for Bishop at the desk and tries him on his cell phone. No answer. He connected himself without Bishop. He has friends now, a number of his own to call.

The rain comes as he sits down to noodles at the café across the street. It's suddenly cooler and the sky darkens. Mike eats slowly and drinks a green-bottled beer, realizing that he is hungover, and becomes daunted because he has to call the number he got from Burton and he is not a real reporter. He is just causing trouble. He wonders what Dorr is doing right now. Maybe Dorr is like his father. Maybe, now that it's evening, Dorr is sitting down with a Scotch on the rocks and reading a favorite novel again. Maybe he is writing a new story. Mike has no idea—Dorr could be doing anything. Mike is sure only that they'll both be surprised if they meet. Fine.

The rain comes in a torrent. The noodle vendors flee the streets with woks held overhead. The café customers slide their chairs under the awnings. The motorcycle taxi drivers lean against the wall and smoke cigarettes. Mike sees the fake-ID guy packing his easel into a suitcase with his pens and razors, and decides suddenly that he must catch him and have a press credential made. No time to get change, so he leaves too much cash on the table and rushes off after the ID guy, who is now disappearing down an alley.

Around the corner the man steps into a doorway. When Mike catches up he sees two old women squatting in a tiny room. Their creased cheeks are red from a small fire.

The old women stare out at him and Mike makes a hurried half-bow and backs away.

Mike walks through the rain to his table at the café. He is soaked. His plate and money and beer are gone. He pulls his chair even farther under the overhang and lights a cigarette.

Then, across the street, he sees Bridget and Paul, and jumps up again. They are walking under a great black umbrella and do not seem surprised to see Mike.

"Khao San Road is not New York," says Bridget. Mike is not sure what she means by that. He's always running into people he knows in New York.

"Where are you going?" asks Mike.

"A sex show," Paul laughs. "Where else on Buddha Day?"

"It's a kind of holiday," Bridget tells Mike. "Everyone is supposed to be in prayer, around little fires. You should come with us."

They are doing a story for an American men's magazine. Paul is the one who got the assignment.

"It's embarrassing," says Bridget, "but it will help finance the animal book."

"Isn't life grand?" says Paul.

It occurs to Mike that they might have meant to run into him.

31

Mike follows Bridget as she navigates her giant umbrella down a narrow alley. The alley is not wide enough for the three of them to walk abreast. It's like walking in a sweating water pipe. Mike is thinking that he would like to go back to his hotel room and sleep. But he also likes being with Bridget.

The bar is shut behind a corrugated metal door, like a garage. And it's paid off tonight, like every night, Bridget explains, Buddha Day or no Buddha Day. This place never gets busted. Just watched. Paul makes a phone call and they wait until the door begins to rise with a grinding sound.

"Get in quickly," Bridget tells Mike.

A yellow light spills out into the gutter, casting a glow on their shoes. Paul squats in first, and Mike follows Bridget as she ducks under the metal curtain that closes on the concrete behind them.

The club is dark with spotlights above a stage. They sit on stools at a raised table. The bar is crowded with Northern Europeans, tall and blond, mostly overweight like at the Grace.

There are also tight groups of Japanese businessmen drinking whiskey at tables close to the stage. The Thai girls are all light and thin as birds. The waitresses are distinguishable from the hookers because their English is less good. The hookers sit between the Japanese businessmen or stand with the Europeans at the bar and sip glasses of sweet cola. The men buy them drink after drink. Occasionally, if the girl is on good terms with the bartender and she looks at him as he pours for her, he will put some whiskey in the drink. Even after they go to a room with a man, they come back to the bar and drink more colas.

At one end of the stage, under hard white light, a Thai woman is reclining on a lawn chair. Mike heard about this in high school. On either side of her, a girl in sequined panties holds one of her ankles. The woman on the chair is naked and Mike looks at her carefully in the lull after Bridget explains the girls' drinks. Her pussy is shaved and Mike tries to gauge his feelings, create some silent understanding with himself. So what? So this is part of my life. I do not want to fuck this woman. I want to, what, save her?

Mike drinks his beer and watches as the woman on the chair makes a squealing noise and thrusts her hips. The girls seem to be pulling her ankles like levers. A dart flies from the woman's vagina across the room into a target. Cheers erupt from the Japanese businessmen. The Europeans at the bar guffaw and the hookers between them laugh politely. Bridget sneaks pictures and Paul goes to the bar for another round. Mike looks at Bridget and decides it might be easier to watch this alone.

The woman shoots another dart from her pussy, this one into a balloon on the other side of the stage. Pop. She puts in another dart and pops another balloon. Paul returns with drinks.

Mike notices a pumped-up young man with a handlebar mustache leaning against the far end of the stage, sipping a beer. He is wearing a sleeveless shirt. Mike sees the tattoos of a South Pacific tribe wrapped around a thick bicep. He is laughing and looks ridiculous, like those models in Dutch beer ads, thinks Mike.

The woman shoots another dart but her aim is off this time and the dart sticks the handlebar man in the arm. The man bellows and drops his beer. Welcome to the tribe, Mike thinks, and wonders how often this kind of thing happens and whether it's part of the show for the *farangs*. Probably not. Holy shit, people are saying, but some are laughing.

The man is yelling, "What the fuck, what the fuck!" The woman in the chair jumps up and disappears behind the bar. The prostitutes look like they are going to cry, their thin faces shaking and pinched. Trouble is coming, maybe, and they are afraid and hope it does not come down on them. They press themselves more tightly to their Japanese businessmen or tall Europeans. Safety with the customers. The customer is always right.

"I would be catching a cab to a hospital," says Bridget, aiming her camera at the handlebar man.

Mike thinks the guy will tell the story only if he doesn't get a disease.

Paul is still laughing when a high voice calls to him from behind. *"Paul,"* the voice flies, and Mike knows he's heard it before. They turn and see Tweety coming toward them from the pool table just behind them. Paul stands and she throws her arms around him. Bridget, too, seems pleased to see Tweety and they kiss on the cheek.

"Have you met Tweety?" Bridget asks Mike.

"We met last night," Mike says. "This morning."

"With Harrison," says Tweety, nodding very brightly.

Mike looks at Tweety and remembers what Harrison told him about her, that she wants to be a writer. He wonders what her story would be if she could write it right now. Mike remembers something else Harrison told him about her, that she is a roamer, a girl who does not belong to a particular club but works several.

"What are you doing here," Tweety asks him, "in this dirty place?"

"Working," Paul volunteers, "on his travel piece."

"Oh, no," Tweety says, giggling.

"And we must have a quote from you," Paul smiles. "Here, why should Americans come to Thailand?"

Tweety deliberates, staring off toward the stage for a moment, and then, with great seriousness, brings her voice down a notch. "Thailand is the most beautiful country in the world."

Mike cannot tell whether she is joking or not, but he knows that they are all playing some kind of game.

Paul and Bridget clap and laugh. Mike makes a study of the pool game so he doesn't have to look at Tweety, but after a moment she leans close to his ear. He can feel her light breath on his neck. She puts her hand on his arm, gripping him as if to tell a secret. He bends down to hear, to be closer to her.

"Can I go home with you tonight?"

There is something in her voice Mike has heard before. From Jane, maybe? He laughs, but feels terrible and hypnotized.

"Thank you," he says, "not me." He smiles the whole time he speaks, as if this were really funny.

Tweety leans closer and asks again using the same words and breathes again into his ear and puts her hand on his thigh. Mike catches Bridget looking away as he laughs again, and says, "No thank you, Tweety."

Tweety pouts and backs off and starts to banter again with Paul, who starts hugging and touching her. Mike shrugs and Tweety smiles meanly at him and puts her hand on Paul's thigh.

Mike tries to watch the pool. Two guys who look like twins start running the table. They are Thai, and distinguishable to Mike only as white T-shirt and blue T-shirt. They hover like dragonflies, and sink or miss at will, yelling in triumph, cracking the balls and disorienting the *farangs*.

Their behavior is "not in Thai character," says Tweety to no one in particular. "Those boys."

Mike wonders if they might be on *yaa baa*.

Suddenly Bridget is whispering in his ear and he can feel her breath the way he felt Tweety's. It startles him.

"Relax, Mr. Mike," she says.

32

On a vacation in California, when Mike was only five or six, the family passed through a ghost town. At least that's how it seemed to Mike. It was really just a small cannery town called Moss Landing. Mike and Lyle both remembered short trawlers bobbing in the oily harbor. It was a Sunday morning, and the main drag was closed up, except for a weird old antique shop and the gas station. Their mother walked in on a whim while their father was getting gas, and the boys followed her.

Mike immediately found the most interesting piece, which was a 1971 Nikon Nikkomat. The camera was in bad shape with what looked like a bullet hole through the casing, small and circular in front and blooming out like a metal flower in the back. Mike put his little finger in the hole and then showed the camera to his mother. She bought it and told the boys not to mention it to their father and gave it to him for his birthday later that summer.

From then on, the camera sat on Mike's father's bookshelf. At first it was out of Mike's reach. When he was tall enough to get it down, he often played with it. When he was older and stopped playing with it, he still took it down and turned it over in his hands. His mother forgot all about it. His father only occasionally looked at it. Of them all, only Mike valued the camera, having spent his childhood pretending to die as a war correspondent shooting combat pictures with it.

33

A uniformed policeman slides in under the metal guard. He is skinny, with a thin mustache, and has a gun on his hip. He narrows his eyes and customers at the bar stiffen. He scratches his chin with his truncheon. The hustlers disappear up the back stairs.

The cop accepts a beer in a coffee mug, bowing slightly. Mike was never afraid of the police until he arrived in Bangkok. He didn't have to be. No cop had ever looked twice at him before. It's different here. He wishes he did not have the ecstasy residue in his blood. But when he looks around at Tweety, he realizes he is nervous about the cop for the wrong reason. Mike fears getting arrested for something he did, when the thing about cops in Bangkok is what Mike is now reading on Tweety's face. Cops here can do whatever they want. But then, after Tweety gets a good look at the cop's face, she is herself again, telling dirty jokes to Paul. Maybe they all know this cop, Mike thinks. Probably.

The hustlers reappear and the *farangs* around the table laugh at their coming and going and coming. The hustlers laugh with them. They have been winning what will be seven thousand baht off some guy from London. Taking turns letting him win, winning it back bigger. The guy is getting frustrated but orders another drink and keeps playing. Finally his American friend says no more games and stands as if to fight with the hustlers, which confuses them. The American is heavy in tapered jeans and cowboy boots.

The hustlers ignore him and play a game between themselves, putting on a show, wielding their cues like long wands. The American asks them where they think they'll be in twenty years, as if that will settle things, or at least make them feel bad. But then one of the hustlers, the better one, gets to talking. He has a daughter. No, he doesn't have a daughter. His fourteen-year-old wife is pregnant, that's it. Made good money tonight. Good money. Lotta fun. Only played at 20 percent. His eyes are whacked out.

The American says fuck you and turns his back to the pool table and starts flirting with Tweety, whom Mike assumes he knows from other nights. Tweety flirts back even though Mike is sure she doesn't want this guy. Something is not right. The American keeps asking Tweety if she wants another drink. She says she has a drink. The American grabs Tweety's arm, lets go, and then grabs it again. Tweety is laughing and wincing at the same time, and says she cannot go home with him. Finally the American gives up, but he wants the last word.

"All right, Tweetybird," he drawls, kissing her hard on the forehead, "that's OK. But don't ever ask me to buy you a drink again."

Mike and Paul both stand up off their bar stools. Bridget backs up a step and readies her camera.

"Do you all hear that?" the American says to the bar, enunciating, not smiling, "I'm never buying her a drink again. As long as she understands that, I'm fine."

"I think she understands," says Bridget.

34

There was one night when everyone in his family went to jail except Mike.

Lyle went first. He was rarely drunk, but sometimes he took walks with a bottle of bourbon, late at night. He enjoyed how the cab headlights seemed to soften at 3 A.M., how the only people he saw on Fifth Avenue were couples coming home. He grew warm, with heavy steps. Have a swig, sit on the fountain in front of the Plaza, stroll into Central Park and take another swig. Sometimes he brooded, especially if his parents had been crazier than usual, but usually he just allowed the city's shapes to float in and out of his mind. He was careful to be discreet and he was lucky.

But that night he got picked up. Public urination, open container. Bad judgment, he knew. But man, he thought, sometimes you just have to go. Everything was so awful when he was drunk and arrested. Worst of all, his parents would have yet another fight over whose fault it was. Lyle looked so down in the yellow fluorescence of the precinct station that the desk sergeant told him, "Don't worry, kid, it's just a fine."

Lyle knew that, just a fine, but when Mike came to pick him up at the station Lyle couldn't stop apologizing.

"What a hassle," he kept saying. "I know it's not a big deal, but what a hassle. Sorry, Mike." Mike didn't want to hear it. He hated when his brother apologized.

Mike insisted on being there with Lyle to explain to their parents the next day.

The boys told their parents at the dinner table. Take-out pizza off fine plates with good red wine and candles, because their parents had just gotten back from Long Island. Mike felt sorry for his brother, who wolfed his pizza and slurped his wine. And Lyle felt worse for Mike because here he was about to wreck it all for his brother, when for once their parents looked OK, even cheerful around the table.

Lyle told them, and Mike added how the cop had said it was no big deal.

"You're a good brother, Mike," said his father. "I just hope you weren't scared," he said to Lyle. And it seemed that was all he would say.

Their mother shook her head, but she was smiling. Mike could see that she would have been angry at other times, but now she wasn't. She almost laughed, and she said to Lyle how low-rent it all was.

"I know," Lyle said, "I'm really embarrassed. It'll never happen again."

"Oh, Lyle," their mother said, "don't worry about it. Your father went to jail for drunk driving last night." And then she blew out all the candles and left the table.

* * *

When they heard, they both imagined one of those green back roads out on Long Island and their parents driving home from a dinner party in some big house. No streetlights, so if their father turned off the headlights by accident when he meant to signal, it would be terrifying for their mother. And she would have a lot to say, in the car. Their parents were not the same in the car as they were at the dinner parties. Probably they had too much to drink. And a cop pulled them over.

The boys were sure there was never any real danger, because their father was a great driver. Both boys had ridden with him after a beer or a few and were never afraid. He would never let anything happen to them or their mother. But then Mike's mother had been so belligerent with the cop, when she saw that he would arrest her husband, that he arrested her too.

35

Mike is woozy from the beer and feels a cold sweat on his neck as he watches Tweety disappear with a squat man in a leather biker vest. Mike wonders if the guy walking up the stairs, holding Tweety's hand, is a dwarf.

"That's her uncle," says Bridget, "and her pimp sometimes. Only family she has in Bangkok, except for a younger brother."

"Little guy," says Mike.

"People are afraid of him. Makes it easier for Tweety to fuck people for money."

"Why are they afraid of him?"

"He's a thug," Bridget says, almost brightly, "from a drug operation up north."

Mike doesn't want to think about Tweety anymore. Dancers are now sliding up and down a row of poles, naked except for purple garters and red feathers in their hair. Mike thinks they look like pistons of flesh going up and down.

The American comes back and Mike watches him tap his pointed boot at the bottom of the stairs, impatient, waiting for something. And then Tweety's pimp uncle is back too, and they are talking. Mike points this out to Bridget, who, he realizes with alarm, is also drunk. She runs her long, pale fingers through her bright red hair and smiles mournfully at Mike.

"Poor Tweety," says Bridget, "she always knows."

"It's her business," says Paul, clearing his throat, "but that American looks awful."

"We should do something tonight," says Bridget. "I'm going to buy her out."

Paul shakes his head as Bridget walks over to the uncle and the American.

"What's she doing?" Mike asks.

"Who knows," says Paul, looking at the ceiling and lighting a cigarette. "Who knows life?"

Mike gets up and follows Bridget. They are all by the wall, in the shadow under the staircase. Mike comes up behind Bridget just as she is saying that she will pay double what the American is paying. The uncle likes Bridget's offer and apologizes to the American, pointing to another girl across the room who might replace Tweety.

"We had a deal," says the American. "I already paid."

The uncle apologizes, but says he is a businessman and offers the money back.

"This is bullshit," says the American. He is sweating and the blood is going to his face and he is stomping his cowboy boots. He even spits on the floor.

"What the fuck are you doing?" he demands, jabbing a finger at Bridget. "You can't have her. You won't even fuck her."

"How do you know?" says Bridget.

Mike notices Tweety, crouching on the staircase, watching.

"Fine, goddammit," says the American. "I'll pay the same."

"Come on," Bridget says, "there are so many other girls here. What difference does it make?"

"Fuck you," says the American. "You want to pay more?"

Bridget doesn't have any more money. She looks at Mike and he nods. His good leather wallet is full of money. He can feel Tweety's eyes on him as he hands it to Bridget. The American yells, "What is this shit?" and starts jabbing his finger at Mike. "She's for you?"

Mike doesn't say anything. The uncle quickly takes Mike's money from Bridget. The American whirls and calls Tweety a little bitch he didn't want to fuck anyway.

When the American turns back to get his money, the uncle is gone.

36

The fight starts like a fight between children, with shouting.

"What kind of con is this?" the American yells, pushing past Bridget and punching Mike clumsily, but with the full force of his shoulder. Mike sees the punch coming. The fist expands until it's all he can see, but he's too slow from the beer to slip it. It hits Mike in the nose and bright red blood flows over his lips as he stumbles back like a tripping dancer.

The cop drinking from the coffee mug sees Mike get punched and puts down his beer. The American is now on top of Mike, clawing into him. Mike feels his heat and weight and the hair on the American's forearms rubbing in the blood on his face. Mike flails his arms, but the American has a hand under his chin and is pushing back, trying to hit him in the temple with his other hand. "Oh shit," Mike hears Bridget say.

Paul starts to pull the American off, but the cop pushes him away and clubs the American hard on the head. Mike hears the cracking sound and coughs on the floor, scrambling to get up as the American blacks out.

The cop chatters furiously at Mike, who doesn't understand.

There is blood, slick and matte in liquid tendrils, dripping down the cop's wooden club. The cop is pushing Mike, and Bridget tells him to just get against the wall. Paul is on his cell phone. The cop cuffs Mike and then puts handcuffs on the American, who is still unconscious on the floor.

The cop scowls at Mike and is taking his radio from his belt when Paul says something in broken Thai to him. A name. He is giving the name of another cop. You know? He is on his way here, wait for him. When the cop hears this he cracks Mike in the spine with his club. The shot feels electric and hot up into Mike's neck. He has done that before, thinks Mike.

The cop orders everyone back. Only Paul is left close enough to Mike and the American to translate. Mike looks at the wall. He can feel his heart pounding and hears the cop and Paul parlaying. He strains to listen. He wishes he could understand the cop's radio. He knows suddenly that his fate crackles along those shortwaves. He wishes that it had all gone differently, but when he looks into the wall, he realizes with a strange surge of happiness that it's all just totally fucked. He imagines the horrors of prison in Thailand. He keeps his eyes open and isn't panicking and this gives him confidence. Let's just see how far it can go, let's see how much trouble a white kid from New York can actually get into. Is there a hole in the world so deep that my father can't track me down and pull me out?

Someone bangs on the metal door. Mike is straining to see, twisting his neck for a sliver of vision behind him.

Another cop has arrived, a lieutenant, and somehow Burton is right behind him. Mike thinks it's as if they came together. He sees them over his shoulder and sees how the lieutenant intimidates the uniformed cop. The lieutenant looks like a pig. This pig lieutenant was my contact, Mike realizes.

The uniformed cop relates what happened with deference to the lieutenant and the lieutenant grunts. Mike feels the flow of the narrative, where the American punched him, where the cop swiftly subdued the troublemakers. Mike darts a look up the stairs, searching for Tweety. She is gone from her perch.

Mike listens to Burton and the lieutenant talking as the cop uncuffs him.

"How's your new son?" asks Burton. "All his sisters taking care of him?"

"I don't like having to come out in the rain," says the lieutenant. "I like to stay dry."

"Of course," says Burton.

"It is too much trouble," says the lieutenant, and he turns abruptly to leave. Everyone in the bar is watching. The uniformed cop looks at the unconscious American and calls for another coffee mug of beer. The lieutenant ducks under the metal door.

Burton claps an arm around Mike's shoulders. No worries. He is smiling and reassuring, but Mike knows he had to use a favor. When Mike starts to apologize, Burton says, "That's what they're for, those kind of favors. I'm just glad everyone was in a good mood. It could have been tricky with that lieutenant." Mike wonders what kind of tricky Burton means.

"Let's go for a drink," Burton says and leads Paul and Mike out the front door of the club. Mike notices that the patrons pretend not to look at him now. He sees their fear of him and his companions, their awe of trouble survivors. He likes it.

Following Burton around the back of the club, Mike sees a wooden staircase to the second floor, crowded with Thai girls. Some are wearing robes. Some at the top by the door, just towels. There must be a dozen smoking and chatting and looking tired like nurses outside an ER.

Paul and Burton smile and say hello to the nearest girls. Before Burton can ask about them, Bridget and Tweety emerge from the door at the top of the stairs. Mike thinks it's strange to see Bridget there. He is even more unsettled by Tweety, who is now wearing simple jeans and a T-shirt, instead of the uniform of the whore. Mike also notices her skin, how clear it looks without makeup, how soft.

"Ready?" says Burton to Tweety.

Tweety nods and smiles without opening her mouth, as if steeling herself for something that will hurt but is good for you, like a shot.

37

Mike's mother took her boys to the Central Park Zoo only once. It was very early on a Saturday morning, and she had woken them up and rushed them out of the house. Even in the rush, Mike saw his father asleep in his suit on the couch in the living room. Mike's mother was pretending to be cheerful, and he and Lyle were both uneasy about this. They didn't know what to say and were careful not to irritate her.

"Relax," she said in a flat voice when they walked into Central Park at Sixty-fourth Street. "We're going to the zoo, not school." She bought them fleshy hot dogs for breakfast from a vendor with a cart, another surprise because they were not allowed to eat street food. Mike and Lyle would remember all of this vividly, because it was unusual to be with their mother any Saturday morning, but mostly because they had then gone to see the polar bear that was famous for being depressed.

Before she saw the animal, their mother didn't know there was anything notable about the bear. She caught her breath and squeezed Mike's shoulder when she saw it. All the fur on both sides of its muzzle was gone, leaving only skin the color of the dark blood beneath it. The three of them watched as the bear walked toward them into the bars of the cage without turning its head until its nose was wedged between the black steel. With deliberate strength the bear planted its haunches and, stiffening its shoulders and neck, began to scrape its muzzle up and down between the bars. The bear's eyes were open the whole time, grinding down its face.

Mike remembered well that after a couple rounds of this his mother looked down at the boys and said, "They should kill that bear."

When they got home, their father had made elaborate sandwiches for lunch. Not long after, their mother read that the bear had lacerated the face of a third zoo keeper and was to be put down. She cut out the clipping and put it on the refrigerator door.

38

Mike is a little off. He can feel it, in his head, behind his eyes. It has just stopped raining—the air feels like breath—and Burton is leading them to a bar called Triple Happiness. Silvery reflections of street lamps steam off the street. Pay attention to the weather, Mike thinks, as he walks between Bridget and Burton. This is what his father always said. Weather makes you smarter, weather doesn't lie, weather is real. Just behind them, Tweety is with Paul, who recounts the adventure. "Isn't life grand?" he says after each twist in the story. Tweety is an obsequious audience, laughing, feigning fear and shock. Mike hardly listens. He thinks he sees a girl on a motorcycle, flying up the street, almost off the ground. It spooks him.

"Did you see that?" he asks Bridget. She didn't.

"You must have got hit hard," she jokes.

"Yeah," he says, "maybe." He thinks it may or may not be his own growing hallucination. He doesn't give it much thought.

Yes he does.

39

Inside Triple Happiness, Mike and Tweety sit across a table from each other. They haven't spoken since they left the sex club. She is especially pretty in the darkness of the bar, all shadows and black hair. From the way she looks at him Mike thinks he is supposed to speak first, but he remains silent.

"Maybe you are like Christopher Dorr," she says.

Mike doesn't know whether she says this because she knows it will get his attention or because it is true or maybe both. Somehow this is the worst thing she could say to him. Maybe it's just the way she said it. She is fucking with him. He knows this for sure.

When the others return with drinks, Tweety gets up and goes to the bar alone.

"I think there might be some kind of confusion with Tweety," Mike says.

"Not your fault," says Burton. "Language problem. It'll get sorted."

Bridget follows Tweety, and Mike tries not to watch. Between them and the girl on the motorcycle, Mike is afraid he wants to fuck every woman he meets in Bangkok. Afraid of what, though? He wasn't afraid to fuck Jane. Burton lights a cigarette and offers him the pack.

"I think Tweety thought I wanted to hire her for the night," Mike says.

"Well that's what you did," Burton chuckles.

"You know what I mean."

"It's not that complicated. Bridget will explain to her."

"That's what she's doing now?"

"It's happened before."

Mike thinks about this. "It wasn't even me," he says. "It was Bridget."

"I know," says Burton.

Paul gets up shaking his head and follows Bridget. Mike wants to ask Burton if Paul has slept with Tweety. Instead he says he doesn't want to piss Paul off.

"What does that mean?" asks Burton levelly and finishes his drink. "Paul's just pissed about the police. I'm telling you, this will all get sorted."

Mike isn't so sure, but then all of them are back at the table and Tweety is laughing and smiling at him. She and Bridget have been to the bathroom. Like high school, thinks Mike.

The plan now is to go to Burton's place and smoke some hash, come down from the night's craziness. And Tweety is coming. Paul and Bridget insist, as if this were a normal thing. Mike doesn't participate in the inviting and neither does Burton, although it's his house, and his hash they are planning to smoke.

40

At Burton's house, they sit on the terrace and pass around a pipe. Tweety is very quiet at first but talks more after she smokes, which makes everyone happy. They all ask her questions, and Tweety tells about how she lives in Khlong Toei and sends money home to her family in the north. She talks about her younger brother working in the city too. He just bought a new motorcycle and this is a big deal. Their village is small and very poor, very remote. She says she understands why the government is killing all the drug users, but Tweety doesn't agree with this. She uses the term "excessive force" like a new appliance she doesn't want to break.

Mike asks Tweety if she has ever taken *yaa baa*. She laughs, very high. "Only take it once," she says. "Made me want to kill a *farang*."

"Who?" asks Mike as a joke, and then realizes his question has made everyone else uneasy.

Mike is now stoned enough on the hash to ask about Dorr again, which is what he really wants. He waits for an opening. The conversation rolls and splits and reconnects. They all talk about how crazy families are. Burton's family shipped him off to boarding school. Bridget's father worked in a zoo. Mike gets to talking about his parents, too, which he knows is not good.

"Same as all the rest," he says, trying to concentrate through the dope but giving away too much, he realizes, as he speaks. "Drunk, crazy. They're old-fashioned about it. Stigma. Shit, they've made it this far."

Mike lights a cigarette and tries to calm himself, determined not to mention the breakdowns, undiagnosed, ignored. "But you have to trust people to take care of themselves," he continues. "It's all just part of the deal."

"Not lost their minds yet?" Bridget wants to know.

"Best training for an artist is an unhappy childhood," says Burton.

That cliché, thinks Mike.

Harrison shows up with a bottle of bourbon. "Is the bar fighter here?" he asks, laughing.

"I would like to see snow," says Tweety.

Bridget and Paul and Burton all want to get out of news and make art and eventually go home, but Tweety would just like to be in some snow. She has never even seen snow, except in movies, and she can't imagine being in it. Specifically, she would like to stand under a snowing sky and look up and catch snowflakes on her tongue.

"The hell with snow, and I'm never going home," says Harrison, stroking the top of his shaved head with one hand and pouring his bourbon with the other. "What about you, Mike?"

"I want to go home, too," he says, "but just to my hotel."
They all laugh.

But suddenly it's as though an alarm clock has gone off in
Tweety. She says she has to leave. She thanks Burton formally.
Watching her get up and collect herself, Mike is again taken
with her body and wonders if maybe he should take her home
with him after all. Tweety smiles at him and says thank you,
very seriously. She extends her hand to him and as they shake
he can feel her softness. She stands at full height and smiles
once more at everybody, then disappears out the door, looking
from behind like a girl Mike might have known back home,
leaving in jeans and a T-shirt after a long party.

41

Mike's father was filled with regret for sleeping with Dorr's sister. He tried to explain his feelings to her, but that only infuriated her. She understood that she was nothing. They never spoke again.

Mike's mother had broken up with Dorr by Christmas. He was too wild, and she thought that maybe she had made the worst mistake of her life. Mike's father would not take her back. She asked Analect to act as an emissary on her behalf. He said he would do what he could but then made a pass at her. He failed, of course.

Dorr moved to another house and he and his sister dropped out of the others' lives. The first news Mike's father got of them, about a month after graduation, was that the sister was back in New Orleans and pregnant. Mike's father wondered what she was going to do with the baby but didn't try to find out, though he was sure it was his.

42

Mike would not remember how Tweety came quietly back into Burton's apartment or her undressing. He would only remember her appearing over him, naked, when he awoke on Burton's couch. Mike was still drunk and high from the hash when she began to undress him, and then he was naked from the waist down. He would remember images, fragments. The slope of her back as she put a condom on him. The veil of her long black hair against his face, and the only thing she said: "You paid for me, now I want to pay you." After that, Mike did not think about anything but her and her body and trying to please her, though he could tell he was like a child to her.

He would not remember her leaving.

43

Mike wakes up sweating in a slant of sunshine on Burton's couch. He sits up, grabs a piece of paper, and starts a note to Burton, but as he is writing it Burton emerges from the bedroom. Through the door, Mike sees Bridget lying in a tangle of sheets. She is beautiful but very distant, like a good oil painting of a nude at the wrong end of a telescope. Burton looks washed and clean in his fresh silk shirt, his blond hair up in the sprouting knot.

"Do you want to stay for breakfast?" Burton asks. "I think I'll make some eggs and things."

Mike explains he has to get back to his hotel. Check messages, find Bishop, do some more reporting for his story. He wants to go to a club or two and ask some more questions and score some drugs to see what deals are like for the backpackers. He's going to walk into the slums on his own.

"Well, good then. Call us later for a drink, yeah?"

"I definitely will."

"Whenever you like. Really."

In fact, Mike has no plans to go anywhere until the next day, when Harrison has promised to introduce him to Christopher Dorr.

Outside, the bright sky presses down on him and he wonders where Tweety is.

44

Leaving his hotel again after a shower, Mike checks reception for messages. None, but there's a sealed envelope waiting for him. He knows who it's from.

He crosses the street to his café and orders a coffee, and eggs on his noodles. He lights a cigarette and waits for his coffee before opening the letter—just something to read, like it could have been the Sunday paper back home.

The note is from Bishop, of course, and briefly apologetic. He says he knows Mike has connected with Burton and that they will all meet up in the next few days to compare notes. "Enjoy yourself and stay out of trouble" is how it ends.

Mike knows he will stay out of trouble. He has found enough for one stupid backpacker story. He has done it. He will go out again tonight with his new friends but now there is no pressure. He has done enough. And so today he releases himself for the afternoon to go and see a *wat*. He will go and see the famous Emerald Buddha. He is sure he will like it. Everyone in his family likes churches even though none of them likes religion. He thinks this makes sense and is fine. *Ritual*. The check comes and Mike takes it with two hands and a quiet thank you, as he has learned to accept things from people as a sign of respect.

45

Until Mike was in junior high school, he said prayers every night before he went to sleep. No one in his family told him to do this or taught him what to say, but he had done it as far back as he could remember.

They weren't really prayers; they were last words. He reasoned, as a little boy, that if he was going to die before morning, he wanted to have chosen his last words. So he did, and said them either out loud or slightly under his breath, depending on whether his brother was awake in the room. Somehow saying the words made them more true.

Mike never mentioned any God in these last words, nor specifics of his life, nor requests. Nothing, really, except a brief and particularly worded affirmation of how he felt about his family and being alive. He never told anybody about this. Lyle knew his brother said something to himself every night, but he never asked about it.

Mike didn't name what he was doing and it didn't occur to him that it was strange until he was in junior high school, and by then he had stopped without thinking about it.

The night before he was to leave for Asia, he said his last words again. He hadn't done it in years, and they just popped into his mouth and embarrassed him, and then he couldn't sleep. So he added to his usual statement: "We are all invincible until the first heart attack."

This is a modern idea.

46

Khao San Road is not as difficult as it was just two days before, but while he is walking to find the *wat,* Mike loses his way. The side streets widen and the heat and dust of the traffic make the walk unpleasant. He stops for a cigarette, watching a soccer game in a park. The boys playing are young, not yet teenagers, and they move like identical insects up and down the field. Mike can't tell them apart, can't pick one to follow. Total *farang,* he thinks.

He walks on and finally sees the spire of the *wat.* It is fine and glinting, piercing up through the smog. He sets out toward it but comes to a six-lane street that moves like a highway. Implacable *tuk-tuk* drivers compete with trucks for the middle lanes and the motorbikes weave and lean between them. The *wat* is on the other side. Mike walks along the highway.

There is nowhere to cross, but Mike sees a young man in work jeans and unlaced boots at the edge of the rushing traffic. The young man watches casually for a moment and then, with a quick first step, begins a controlled jog through the traffic.

Mike stops short, sure that the young man is going to get hit as he disappears behind a bus. Mike hears squeals and blares. But then the bus passes and the man is on the other side of the highway walking easily away. Mike thinks about it but decides he is not that crazy. It's not for *farangs*.

Mike has been passing in front of what he guesses are civic buildings, pale and ugly, but now, just behind him, he realizes, is the National Gallery. The building is unremarkable and un-advertised but for a small sign on the door. Air-conditioning leaks from the entrance and Mike wants to get out of the heat.

In the antechamber a sleepy woman in braids behind an information counter points to a sign in English with a price. Mike usually buys everything with overlarge denominations, which is easier than sorting out the unfamiliar currency. Here, though, alone with the sleepy woman, he is unhurried, so he works out the amount and walks into the cool silence of the museum.

Arranged in the first room are rows of white and bald mannequins, taller than any of the Thai women Mike has met. They are dressed in long ball gowns, strange high couture. The fashion is bad, like wardrobe mistakes from period Hollywood movies. Some of the mannequins have enormous headdresses; others are belted with sequined patterns of birds or flowers. The colors are the palette of stained glass, muted as though overwashed. Mike thinks of St. John the Divine, back in New York, and the strange halos he saw in the dark church as a child.

Some of the dresses are revealing. The mannequin breasts stand straight out and hold up some of the dresses. One dress, hung with purple feathers, is cut from clavicle to crotch, and Mike gently pulls the fabric back into place, to cover an erect nipple.

All the mannequins face in the same direction and Mike thinks of a discovery somewhere in Africa that his father once told him about. An archaeologist had found eight huge cat heads arranged in burial, all pointing the same way, which was evidence, he said, of early religion. Pagan rites of the Upper Neolithic, when there was more than one breed of man. Jane had told him that arranging the cat heads must have been a moment of great transformation, like the first painting on a cave wall, the beginning of sedentary life. The breakthrough. Not the same thing with the mannequins, but air-conditioned, at least.

The silence is broken by giggles, and into the room slouches a wide-bellied young man with wild copper hair and his arm around a pierced, pale girl in dark lipstick and a leather skirt. They are laughing about something and seem high. Seeing Mike they quiet and the young man stifles another laugh. His shirt has a skull with a snake wrapping through the eye sockets printed on it and is faded and sweat-stained.

Mike decides to engage them.

"Strange, huh?" Mike waves at the plastic fashion formation.

The skull boy just stares at him.

"Strange, these I mean," Mike repeats and this time Skull Boy pulls on Pierced Girl and points to Mike, saying something to her quickly in a romance language that Mike can't quite place.

"Oh yes, very strange," says Pierced Girl. "I am sorry my friend does not speak English." Pierced Girl's voice is a slow and breathy soprano and accented. French, maybe.

"Did you come for the exhibit?" Mike asks, though he sees they have only stumbled in like himself.

"Oh no, we only were hot and could not cross the highway." She says *highway* as if it were two words and a question.

"But I think they are wonderful," she says and starts moving from dress to dress, feeling the fabric of each between her thumb and forefinger.

"What brings you to Bangkok?" asks Mike.

"We are only tourists," smiles the girl. "We have been to the clubs and things."

These kids will be easy, Mike thinks.

"I've been meaning to get to the clubs too," he says. "You know any good ones?"

"Oh yes," she says. "We go every night. He loves the clubs, but I have to make him come to places in the day." She pauses to speak to Skull Boy in their language and he raises his eyebrows and Mike thinks he catches the word *droges.*

"Have you seen drugs in the clubs?"

Pierced Girl laughs and immediately relates the question to Skull Boy, who laughs harder.

"Oh yes, drugs everywhere," she says in a fake whisper. "This is the place for it. Vacation, no?" She has taken a silver ring out of her nose and is holding it up to the nose of a mannequin in a yellow fishnet bodysuit. "She is better than the Emerald Buddha, no?"

"Did you like the *wats*?" asks Mike. "I wanted to see the one across the highway, too."

Pierced Girl gives the mannequin a kiss on the lips. Skull Boy is rocking another of the plastic women on her heels and he calls out an idea to Pierced Girl and she laughs.

"What did he say?"

"He said we should knock one over and let them all fall on one another, how do you say it, like ah . . ."

"Dominoes," says Mike.

Skull Boy is trying to impress her and she is rolling her eyes but smiling. He is going to do it. Mike instinctively looks to see if there is a guard or a cop, even though he knows there are none in the gallery. Skull Boy rocks and rocks and then the quiet of gallery is violated by a cacophony of crashing plastic women.

47

Lyle once disappeared for two days. It was August.

Mike had half awoken to shouting in the night. The next morning when he went downstairs he saw the antique kitchen mirror lying shattered on the floor, an unripe pineapple among the shards, as though thrown from the bowl of fruit on the counter. Lyle and one of the cars were gone all day. When Mike called his cell phone it rang in on the hall table. Mike was sure his brother was safe—Lyle was supremely competent and a good driver—but this was strange.

His father did not descend from his bedroom until late in the afternoon. Mike stayed out of the kitchen, and didn't speak to his father until the mirror was cleaned up. His mother arrived back home in the evening, explaining that she had gotten up early and had been running errands all day. No one said anything about the mirror or the pineapple.

By dinnertime, Mike could see his parents were anxious about Lyle. But somehow not anxious enough. Like they knew what was happening. The big house felt hot and close. Mike took a long walk on the beach before he went to bed, and just because he had always been curious and was feeling eerie and frustrated, he kneeled down at the shore and drank some sea-water from his cupped hands, just to see what it was like.

The next morning, Lyle had still not come home. Mike's mother called all of Lyle's friends, who said they didn't know where he was. By that afternoon, she was becoming hysterical, but Mike's father calmed her down. Mike didn't know how. They gave Lyle another day.

Lyle came home in time for dinner. He didn't explain where he had been, and his mother, whom Mike suspected had been coached by his father, knew enough not to ask. When they were sitting down to eat, Lyle reached down next to the table and picked up a shard of mirror, missed in the cleanup, and looked at his parents before tossing it in a perfect three-point arc into the tall white kitchen garbage can.

Later that night when Mike asked his brother what had happened, Lyle said, "Seven years bad luck."

48

The three of them run out of the gallery, into the sudden heat and around a corner, where they finally stop. Skull Boy is still laughing as they catch their breath. Mike can see that this will be a high point of his trip. After a moment Skull Boy begins walking away, but Pierced Girl lingers, looking at Mike. Skull Boy calls to her. Mike doesn't understand what he says but he can tell Skull Boy wants Pierced Girl to himself.

"OK, OK," she says, but then she asks Mike if he would like to get a drink.

Mike, caught off guard, says, "Sure."

"Come then."

"I have to be somewhere," he lies. "I was only killing time."

"Tonight?"

"Sure, thanks."

"Do you know Chart?"

"Near Khao San Road?"

Mike doesn't know Chart but of course it's near Khao San Road. Maybe he'll go, but Pierced Girl isn't even that pretty.

For the hell of it, he asks her if she's heard of a Christopher Dorr.

"We don't remember anyone's names," she tells him.

Mike looks at the *wat* spire across the highway and turns to walk back to his hotel, wishing he had seen the Emerald Buddha.

49

Mike's father wore a long, black overcoat, and Mike held on to his coattails as they walked up the steps of the cathedral. He remembered the view of the gray, stone building ahead of them over his father's shoulder. Lyle was older and bounded up the wide snowy steps. He was in a hurry. "The faster we go to bed," he explained to Mike, "the faster we wake up."

Their mother said their father shouldn't make them go to church.

"Would you like to come?" he asked her.

"Would you like to come to the party?" she asked him.

She was going to a Christmas Eve party on Fifth Avenue. The deal was they would all meet back at home before midnight. That was reasonable, and by reasonable compromise they would prosper and not be crazy. So what if they weren't together all the time.

"Holidays are arbitrary," their father told them, though Mike knew he was lying to make everybody feel better. "Ritual is important for a reason."

50

Back at the hotel, Mike takes a cold shower and thinks about how there is no way he is going to Chart. Three days ago he would have forced himself, for the story, but the story is bullshit, or at least it's a different story now. It's not about backpacker kids eating pills. It's about *farangs* not knowing anything and getting in trouble. It's about me. And sometimes *farangs* ought to stay in their hotel rooms.

When the phone rings, Mike stays in the shower. If it's Burton let him think I'm out, Mike tells himself. I said I would be out. The phone stops and doesn't ring again. Wasn't even important.

He lies naked on the bed watching international news to kill the hours. The news is strange and accented, much different from American news, more interesting. A bomb explodes in Moscow and no one takes responsibility. Police clash with rebels in Haiti and the voodoo priests chuckle in the alleys and dance in the moonlight. A baby with two heads dies in Santo Domingo even though two-headed baby experts fly in from around the world. Mike falls asleep as the program starts to loop.

He wakes up at eleven. So much for Pierced Girl. He wants to go back to sleep but is hungry and decides to go to the McDonald's in the lobby of the hotel. A total *farang* move.

On his way downstairs, Mike stops by Bishop's door and listens. He wonders where Bishop actually is. Maybe his "best girl" is a wife and he has a whole family in Bangkok that has never seen his skyscraper apartment in Hong Kong. More likely Bishop is in some teak house with a thirteen-year-old hooker. Mike hears nothing through the door.

Eating his double cheeseburger, Mike continues to mull over Bishop, who, he decides, is behaving badly. There is a code and Bishop is not following it. Analect will not like the way Bishop disappeared. Analect lives by this code, Mike is sure. The same code his father lives by. It's about action. It's about always doing your job, before anything else. Mike overheard his father tell his mother this many times, when she complained that he was working too hard. Bishop is not doing his job, Mike thinks, so he is an asshole.

Assholes everywhere, actually. An American boy, about Mike's age, is telling the Thai girl with acne behind the counter that he doesn't want any pickles.

"I said I don't want any pickles." The kid is getting louder.

The girl hands him his tray with both hands and a slight bow. The kid notices Mike watching and comes over and sits down.

"See?" He lifts the bun, shows Mike the pickles on his cheeseburger, and pulls them off with venom. Mike shrugs. The kid tells him he is headed to a full moon party on the beach, but he's heard they've been checking for drugs on the way in. "It fucking sucks," he says.

Looking at this kid, Mike thinks about codes. Analect and his father, in adjacent prison cells, tapping their knuckles to the bloody bone on cinderblock walls. Secret language. A formalized system of deception, thinks Mike. Codes cover the truth. Like all of his father's talk about action. Like Tweety's makeup.

Then Mike stops thinking because Tweety walks in. She spots him and walks over. The asshole kid stops chewing.

"I like Big Macs," she says. "Can we get one and go to your room?"

51

"Sex doesn't matter," Tweety says. "Not important anymore." Mike and Tweety sit side by side on the edge of his bed. She is eating her Big Mac.

"We're even now," she says between bites. "Maybe you can help me." She is so slight that watching her devour the enormous Big Mac makes her seem grotesque to Mike.

"I'll try," Mike says. "What do you need help with?"

"I don't want to work for Harrison anymore. Or Mickey Burton. Can I work for you?"

"I can't hire you, Tweety. I don't even have a real job."

"Can you get me a job like yours?"

Mike thinks of how he got his job. How it started thirty years ago between Analect and his father.

"I don't know," says Mike.

"They won't let me quit."

"Harrison?"

"You tell them to leave me alone, please. I want to stay home."

And then Tweety stands up and, before Mike can say anything, puts the rest of her Big Mac in her purse and is gone.

52

In Hong Kong, as soon as he knew he was going to Bangkok, Mike looked up Christopher Dorr on the Internet. He sat in his cubicle in the gleaming, carpeted magazine office and read everything he could find. Christopher Ames Dorr was educated at St. Bernard's and Exeter and Harvard and, finally, Oxford, in East Asian Studies. He had won numerous awards for his investigative pieces, and was most famous for a cover story about the Wa people who farmed opium for a Burmese warlord cartel along the northern Thai border. Mike read the piece and had printed a copy to take with him. It was so close to the culture it was almost as if Dorr were Wa himself.

On the contributors page, Dorr was characterized as a fearless journalist who had been everywhere. Mike also found two photographs. In the first, Dorr stood at the edge of a Harvard boxing team picture. Mike's father was in the same picture. The second was a photograph of Dorr standing with some villagers in a remote field. The credit, Mike had noted, when he looked at the article again, in Bangkok, was Harrison Stirrat.

Mike has meant to ask Harrison about the picture for days now. He doesn't know why he hasn't. Having kept it to himself for so long, it now feels like a bad secret. And now he has another, about Tweety.

53

Mike wakes up to knocking on his door, three very sharp raps that yank him from sleep. It's Harrison, who says he called the room last night but there was no answer.

Mike dresses as fast as he can and follows Harrison down the stairs. They cross Khao San Road like they own it. Harrison doesn't look twice at anything. When they get to his clean, blue motorcycle, Harrison tells Mike there's been a change of plans. Dorr lives in Khlong Toei, in Tweety's neighborhood, and Harrison has to see her, so they can leave together when Mike is done talking to Dorr. Good, thinks Mike. A ride out.

"Have to," says Harrison, with an edge in his voice. "Tweety changed the plan."

"What happened?" asks Mike as he climbs on the back of the bike.

"I have to talk to her. We don't want it to get tricky."

Mike wonders about that word.

Harrison glances back at Mike over his shoulder. "She's backing out of introducing us to her brother. Very stupid."

This doesn't feel right to Mike but before he can say anything Harrison starts the engine and drowns out the possibility of further conversation.

The motorcycle trip is long but it goes by too fast for Mike. As they ride into Khlong Toei the tenements give way to tin shanties and squat wooden houses, some separated by broken chain-link fence. The sun is very hot, reflecting off the cracked concrete streets. When they slow down, the neighborhood smells of fruit and motor oil. There are dogs everywhere, in packs and running alone, and Mike hears roosters crowing somewhere nearby. Harrison doesn't turn off the engine when they stop.

Christopher Dorr's square house rises on stilts among the shacks and shanties. The windows are closed with gray wooden shutters.

At least Harrison will be making the introduction.

But then he doesn't.

"Just knock," Harrison tells him.

"You're sure he's home?" Mike can hear the hesitation in his own voice.

"He's always home. Just keep knocking. I'll be the next street over." Harrison points up the road. A toothless woman, not that old, crabs by them on deformed feet as Mike gets off the bike. She looks at him suspiciously. Off in the distance Mike can see the spire of a *wat*.

"Just come to the motorcycle when you're done," says Harrison. "You'll see it. Or I'll be done first and come back here."

Harrison adjusts himself on the bike and looks at Mike, who is looking up at Dorr's house.

"You sure about this?" asks Harrison.

Mike says he is, and Harrison speeds off on his blue motorcycle, disappearing around the corner, leaving Mike standing alone with his many questions in front of Dorr's house.

What the fuck, Mike thinks, we went to the same college.

54

Mike's father talked a lot about how he was looking forward to visiting Harvard now that Mike went there, but when he arrived Mike noticed that he didn't talk very much. It was like the school reminded him of something he hadn't expected to think about, and whatever it was disarmed him.

Mike's father wanted to take a walk by the river, so they walked down there. It had to do with his parents' marriage.

Mike's father and mother got back together four years after graduation. Mike's father had been in Vietnam and was back at Harvard attending business school. Mike's mother was doing PR in New York, mostly for nonprofits. When she heard that he was back in Cambridge she went and convinced him that it made sense for them to be together.

He had been having a hard semester. He wasn't sure that business school was right. His father's family had forced him into it, really. And he wasn't sure that he should have forgiven

Mike's mother. His life seemed impermanent, somehow, and he was worried that it wasn't his own.

One cold fall day when he was particularly uneasy, he sat by the river on a bench and brooded, chain-smoking and gouging a pocketknife into the wood as he sat there. He found that the knife was making letters, and he found that he was carving "Will you marry me?" into the bench. Somehow it made sense.

It was corny, the way he proposed, and he was embarrassed later when she would tell the story, which she was good at telling and liked to tell. In the clear late November air, he showed Mike's mother the writing by the light of his Zippo lighter.

She looked at the carving and said, "Will you try to quit smoking?" She didn't like cigarettes and heavy boozing.

"Anything," he said.

"We're going to be the best," she said, and was sure they would conquer everything. No children for a while, though; it was going to be just the two of them.

Mike's father left his pack of cigarettes there on the bench that night. He didn't quit, though, and his new fiancée picked up the habit from him.

Analect was in Europe working for the *Herald Tribune* when he found out. He had gone to Vietnam, too, but then went to Europe instead of business school. So he came back for the wedding and was the best man. Thereafter he kept in touch with Mike's mother and father as his career accelerated through various editing slots. He also kept in touch with Dorr, who had already made a name for himself, first in Vietnam and then in the Middle East, where he had won a Pulitzer during Black September. Shortly after the wedding, Dorr sent Analect a cruel postcard from Beirut that read, "I got the Pulitzer. I hear he got the girl. How are you, Elliot?"

Analect's occasional visits to Mike's parents always had an edge. No one ever discussed Dorr. Years later, when Analect took over the bureau in Asia, he didn't tell Mike's parents that he was now Dorr's boss. Even when Mike's father called to ask about an internship for Mike. Analect said to send the kid over. And then he sent Mike to find Dorr.

55

Mike walks up the wooden stairs, carefully stepping over rotted planks. Three cats that were sunning scatter up to the porch ahead of him. The porch is small and crowded. There's a rusted motorbike half-hidden under a mildewed yellow tarp and a baby carriage with no wheels. Garbage cans askew. Flies. The cats dodge in and out of the garbage.

From Dorr's porch, Mike has a view of the neighborhood, an expanse of rusted, corrugated roofs glancing sunlight. Between them he can see children and dogs and clotheslines. Across the street, three men in beaten lawn chairs watch his progress up the stairs. They look at him looking at their neighborhood.

Mike turns to the door, kicking over a dog's water dish. The dish is yellow plastic with the name Carrie painted on it by hand. Mike steps over the dish and knocks on the door. There is no answer. He'll be home, Harrison said, just keep knocking. Mike tries again. He feels the eyes of the men across the street as he keeps knocking.

Silence.

Mike wants to leave. His instinct is to get away from this place. His heart pounds. He focuses. He raps three times. Silence. He waits and listens and finds himself holding his breath. He raps three more times, makes himself breathe. Finally, through the silence, he hears shuffling. A bolt slides but the door remains closed.

"Mr. Dorr? My name is Mike. I think Elliot Analect might have written to you from the magazine."

Mike thinks he can feel anger on the other side of the door as he hears another bolt sliding. Suddenly, the door opens and Mike is facing enormous black sunglasses wrapped around a gaunt head.

"Mr. Dorr?" When Mike extends his hand the man salutes him ironically and smiles.

"You're all the way here," says Dorr, sounding high. He gestures for Mike to come in.

Mike steps through the doorway, blinded momentarily by the darkness. Like ink, he thinks, blinking into it. After closing the door behind them, Dorr takes off the glasses and moves slowly to a ripped black leather chair. Even in the darkness, Mike can make out the man's startlingly round blue eyes. The floor is cheap linoleum and Mike hears the scraping again and sees a dog, some kind of Lab mix, turning in tight circles in a corner, dragging her hind feet on the floor. Carrie, Mike figures.

Dorr sprawls in the chair with his legs out before him, his dark shirt open down the front but buttoned at the wrists. Mike waits for the never-coming invitation to sit down and then sets himself, almost perching, on a ragged sofa across from Dorr.

Between them a glass coffee table is covered with dirty plates, glasses, and an overflowing ashtray fashioned out of some kind of bone. This could be the room of any drunk, Mike thinks, or any junkie. Dorr searches the table for something but gives up quickly.

"Will you give me a cigarette?" His voice is slow and smooth. Mike hands him his pack. Dorr puts his sunglasses back on and lights a cigarette. The flicker of the match illuminates the room for a moment, and Mike sees his reflection in Dorr's dark lenses. The dog is still scrabbling in the corner. It will not sit still. The room smells of dog and old food and now, momentarily, the sulfur of the lit match. Dorr takes off his sunglasses again and drops them heavily on the table between them.

"So Elliot Analect sent you to check up on me," he says.

"He just said he thought it would be good if Bishop and I came to say hello."

"Bishop?" Dorr almost laughs. "Bishop's afraid of me. He's probably off fucking some eleven-year-old."

"I haven't seen much of him since we've been here."

"He left you behind, yes?"

"Not really."

"Yes, left behind. Worse places to be left behind, though. Even make a life here." Dorr places the pack of cigarettes carefully on the table. "Have everything you like. Fuck a different child every day of the week. The children you make and the children you fuck, yes? The closer they are together the longer it all lasts."

Mike reaches for a cigarette.

"So how's Elliot?" Dorr exhales blue smoke.

"I don't really know, you know, I'm just an intern."

"Just an intern?" Dorr laughs out loud and the sound dissolves into hacking coughs.

"Harrison Stirrat brought me here," Mike says, and Dorr laughs and coughs again even harder.

56

"You're perfect," Dorr says to Mike and leans forward in his chair, the smoke rising between them. "You should be photographing yourself." Dorr frames Mike in a rectangle between his hands. "Shrewd Elliot. Clever, clever editor. You are your own story. That's what he's after."

Mike is about to say he's not a photographer when he hears the dog whimper again and looks to see it squatting as if about to defecate in the corner. In the next instant Mike knows she is giving birth.

A newborn pup slides from the mother and drops onto the dusty linoleum with a wet sound. She chews the umbilical cord, leaving a green and red shred hanging from the pup, but she doesn't chew the pup out of the sac. It must be her first litter. The pup begins to suffocate. The mother faces the corner again, hind legs spread, shaking and lowing, pushing out the next pup. Mike looks up to see Dorr watching the first pup dying on the linoleum. He moves his eyes to Mike. This is too much, Mike thinks, Dorr is fucking with me. Mike is stiff with nerves as the smell of birth rises from the corner.

Dorr keeps staring at him and begins to groan and speak, sounding sick or falling asleep or both. "I've seen birth, you know, my own sister, she died in childbirth. Because she got knocked up by a friend of mine from college who was too weak to take care of her. Sick, isn't it? Watching your sister die in a fancy New Orleans hospital room because nobody wanted to be there and nobody wanted that kid, they couldn't stop her hemorrhaging . . ."

Mike is frozen. He knows he won't tell Dorr who his father is. It must be him. Carrie drops another black pup onto the ground by the first ones. It can't be my father, Mike thinks, he wouldn't have taken off. Or I would have two brothers.

Dorr's cigarette is burned to the filter. He drops it into the ashtray. "Of course the kid survived. I gave him up for adoption. And you know what? I've seen harsher births, and I know that it's pointless to intervene. I walked into the jungle. There are still native people, *injuns,* simple savage farmers. Maybe working for the Burmese, maybe not. People of superstition, people of the jungle."

Dorr lights another cigarette, and Mike sees his reflection again. "I went with the tribe. Everyone was stoned. Fuck the rice, just smoke all day. And there was a girl, thirteen, fourteen, barely a woman. And I loved her, told her that she could leave the tribe, the People's Army, ha, if she wanted to. And I fucked her, and I stayed for months, working, writing a story. And of course she became pregnant and got herself married while she still could, which was good and lucky. And I fucked her again and again outside in the fields . . ."

Dorr is picking and ripping the leather from the chair with his fingernails. "What about that, yes? And the child was born just close enough for everyone to believe it was the husband's baby, and yellow enough so it wasn't obviously mine. Harrison was with me by then, for the story, and we had become everyone's friend with cigarettes and bubble gum and had smoked dope with them in the very dew of that morning. And as soon as the baby was born and they saw it was a girl, my girl, they took her, and her mother was delirious with pain, even through the opium, sitting on a woven chair with her legs spread wide and the midwife holding her down, because she knew. And I knew and she is screaming at me to stop them. But there was no place for a girl, and so they took her and we followed the man who thought he was the father and his own father into the very field where I had fucked that baby into existence, and I watched my baby girl kicking out as they dug a hole in the brown dirt and covered her up."

"I hope you didn't come expecting to get high," Dorr says now.

Mike just shakes his head.

"I wasn't offering. So don't go presuming. Unless you've got something to trade."

The dog barks short and loud at her litter. She has birthed the last. Puppies squirm on the floor, in their sacs, like disconnected segments of a centipede. The mother stands away, eyeing them suspiciously, tongue out, panting. Dorr is transfixed, watching to see what she will do. Whether she will chew any of the pups out into life, or let them die, or eat one of them as new mothers do sometimes. Or what.

"I have to be going," says Mike, rising carefully.

"And you know, the girl got out," he says almost laughing, "lives here now, up the road." Dorr doesn't take his eyes off the dog. "What are you going to tell Elliot?"

Mike's throat sticks, and Dorr speaks again before Mike can say anything.

"Will you give me your pack of cigarettes?"

Mike checks his shirt then plunges his hands into his pants pockets, searching, searching, but he cannot find the pack. He can feel Dorr's eyes move from the dog to him, moving up and down him as he searches for the cigarettes.

"Oh, look," says Dorr, reaching for the pack, left on the table, "you already gave it to me."

Mike is out the door.

57

Mike's heart is pounding. He trips over Carrie's bowl on the porch again and stumbles down the stairs. He takes off up the street without thinking. He is sweating and the stray animals smell the birth on him and are curious. The men in the lawnchairs watch and smoke. Mike turns at the corner where Harrison disappeared and at the end of the street sees the clean blue bike out of place among the rusted locals in the turnaround.

Mike hears domestic life as he walks toward the bike. A woman singing, the gurgle of water in a sink through the thin walls. He tries to take in everything, observe carefully, calm down. The singing continues. He waits by the bike. There is life on this street. A man crosses in front of him carrying a box full of yellow transistor radios. A woman beats a rug against a low brick wall, exploding motes into the sunlight. Children run in and out of a garage where young men work on motorcycles. Almost hidden at the mouth of an alley, an old man draws water into a bucket from a rusty pump shaped like an elephant's trunk.

Dorr is full of shit, Mike thinks.

* * *

Mike is already tired of waiting. He wants to see the street from a motorcycle, on the way out, or on canvas, not be stuck in the middle of it. It feels like he has already been here a long time. He waits and waits, and the sun crosses the sky slowly, burning him. He tries to watch the neighborhood but knows they are all looking at him. *Farang*. He catches a child, a little girl he thinks, peeking at him through the window of the house. She disappears below the sill. This is Tweety's house, he is sure of it. He wonders how long he has been waiting. He wants to find Harrison and leave. Maybe he should knock on the door of the house. Tweety's house. But then Mike sees Harrison, Tweety, and a young man who he thinks must be Tweety's brother coming toward him from around the side of the house. Behind them are four police officers with drawn pistols. Harrison tells Mike to be calm, to let him do the talking, that everything will get sorted. Mike does not believe this. He can tell by the way the cops are holding their pistols.

From behind him, Mike hears a voice he recognizes. It's the lieutenant from the bar, who cocks his head and tells Mike he does not think it is a very good idea for them to all be getting together like this again. The lieutenant thinks this is funny, but it's not funny at all to Mike. He remembers the feel of the handcuffs coming off, and hearing the lieutenant say something to Burton about wanting to stay dry.

Harrison tells the lieutenant that they've actually met before, too, that he's a friend of Burton's, that they're all friends and all do a lot of business together. The lieutenant seems to consider this for a moment, and tells Harrison to take the young *farang* and get on his motorcycle and leave. He says it is bad business to be friends with *yaa baa* dealers. And tell Burton, he says, there are going to be more changes.

The brother starts crying. Mike looks at Tweety. Her face is hard.

Sometimes life is very simple, is how Harrison explained it. They could stay and die with Tweety and her brother, or leave, and live, speeding away on the blue motorcycle when they hear the shots.

58

In the café across from his hotel, Mike and Harrison sit over beers, both of them staring out at Khao San Road. They sit in silence. Mike is waiting for Harrison to say something, anything.

"That was her brother," is all Harrison says.

Mike knew that.

"Tweety wasn't Thai," Harrison continues. "She was Wa, from the north. Her family lives in the jungle. They're opium farmers. She got out."

"What happens now?"

"Nothing," says Harrison. "We had nothing to do with it."

Mike begins to feel sick.

"We'll get another beer later," says Harrison. He stands up, pulling money from his pocket to pay for his drink.

Mike throws up and has terrible diarrhea in the cramped bathroom. He leans his head on the wall as he sits on the toilet and tries to calm down. He doesn't know what to think. Yes he does.

He thinks about meeting Tweety in the Grace. Buying her out. Getting stoned with her. But in the end there's only one track in Mike's mind and it's numb and floating him to a very bad place.

59

When he returns to the table Mike is not so sick anymore, just empty. It's early evening. He sat there for an hour with Harrison, and now he will sit by himself, drinking beer until long after dark. He stares out at the other *farangs* as they pass by in the fading light.

Mike doesn't know how long he has been there when he notices Dreads and Hardy and Pierced Girl sit down at the Italian café next door. They don't see him. He watches the three of them order beers and pizza. Then Hardy takes out a corncob pipe and lights up. Mike catches the sweet smell of hash right away. Hardy and Dreads furtively pass it back and forth several times, and then Hardy quickly puts the pipe away again. Pierced Girl thinks this is hilarious. They are all still laughing when their first beers arrive. After a little while Mike doesn't watch them anymore.

He knows how the rest of his time in Bangkok will be. He will sit at this table drinking beer, watching *farangs*. Burton will hear about what has happened and come by and find him. Bridget might show up and tell him to relax. Harrison said they'd have another beer, but they won't. Harrison will just be gone. And eventually, Bishop will show up at Mike's table and ask for the stony backpacker quotes to patch together, and that will be the story. Mike never wants to see any of them again.

When he gets back to his room he is sick again and vomits until there is nothing left, but he doesn't pass out. He calls his brother without looking at the time or thinking about the charge to the magazine. He can't get through at first and tears well in his eyes.

Finally he gets a ring and he takes a deep breath and lies on his back on the bed, pressing the phone tightly to his ear. The receiver magnifies his breathing. But the phone just rings and rings until Lyle's voice mail picks up.

"This is Lyle. Leave a message."

Mike hangs up. He is suddenly relieved his brother didn't answer. There is nothing to say.

PART II

Lyle was surprised by how loud the fire was as he ran out of the house.

As it engulfed the living room, the piano caught, and the strings snapped with sharp pings as the wooden frame softened and collapsed. The bookshelves burned from the bottom up, the big art books first, then the middle shelves of hardcovers, and as the shelves collapsed, the cheap paperbacks fell into the conflagration. All the food in the kitchen cabinets burned and the aerosol cans under the sink exploded. On the big dining room table where his father had been studying it, a map of Hong Kong curled and disintegrated into ash. A box of bullets discharged in his mother's bedroom.

The whole house came down in a huge roar, like a jet taking off.

The neighbors found Lyle in shock on the grass, his arms and back smoking. They covered him with a blanket as he lay there, staring up into the stars. When the fire trucks and ambulance arrived, the reflected red and blue of their sirens mixed with the firelight.

He thought of nothing.

60

Mike is all the way uptown, across the street from the Cathedral of St. John the Divine, when American Airlines Flight 11 crashes into the north tower of the World Trade Center.

He is in a coffee shop, buying a blueberry muffin on his way to class at Columbia, where he transferred to after Bangkok. The guy behind the counter turns up the sound and everyone in the place is quiet, watching. No one can believe it. It's like an awful movie, and the people in the coffee shop stare at the TV together in a rapport of horror and international policy analysis. Mike remains silent. He is thinking, as the footage is replayed, that he has to go down there to get his brother. He hopes Lyle hasn't gone in for a closer look or to try to help. Both would be Lyle's way.

Outside the coffee shop, Mike looks downtown into the sky. He saw an oil-thick plume of smoke on the TV, but outside he sees only clear blue. He pictures Lyle watching the news in his apartment and deciding to walk the few blocks to the World Trade Center. This is how Mike thinks now. He can often see things when he thinks them. Especially on this clear morning when he thinks of his brother, spacey and irresponsible, all the way downtown.

A year ago, during his time in Bangkok, someone told Mike, "It's always too early for dread." Mike remembers this and it calms him a little as he considers how he will get to his brother. Lyle's apartment is several blocks from the towers and the plane didn't hit his building. But then Mike thinks maybe it would be for the best if it had. Blow Lyle into sleep. *Me, too.*

Mike and Lyle are orphans. A little over a year ago, their parents died in a house fire and Lyle lost his mind. Mike was in Hong Kong at the time, just returned from Bangkok. Elliot Analect broke the news and flew him home first-class.

Mike scattered his parents' ashes from their old wooden canoe on the bay where they had taught him and his brother to swim. Lyle went into treatment at Pine Hill for post-traumatic stress disorder. After six months he was released, on heavy medication, into the ostensibly normal life that Mike has been protecting ever since. That was why he transferred to Columbia. The months Lyle was in Pine Hill were the most horrifying of their lives. Even on bright days it was always the middle of the night. That was the joke they made up about how it felt, but they both walked as dead boys, even though one was still free.

Mike wonders if Lyle is hallucinating now. He has been hallucinating ever since the fire. Lyle's hallucination, continuing but hidden since his release, is a third brother. Mike hates the new brother. Mike can see him in his own head now, too, knows that he looks something like himself and thinks about putting a bullet through each of his eyes. Lyle accused the false brother of burning down the house, and Mike knows he is still around, even though they both pretend he isn't. Of course Mike doesn't tell anybody. They'd lock Lyle up again. They don't talk about it, and they used to talk about everything. Mike takes out his cell phone and calls his brother.

"This is Lyle. Leave a message."

Mike tells him to stay put unless the shit is right on top of him and that he's on his way. Mike stops himself from saying *to get you*.

61

"My brother burned down our house and killed our parents," Lyle repeated over and over. It was like a mantra.

And this is what Lyle was saying to the doctor when Mike arrived to visit him that first time at the Pine Hill Recovery Center, halfway between New York and Boston. Lyle was drugged.

"He was ruthless," said Lyle.

The doctor held up a hand for Mike to wait at the edge of the room. Mike smiled at his brother from the door. He didn't understand what Lyle was saying, and he didn't want to stand at the bed and look into his red, shot-out eyes.

"Mike," said the doctor, "why don't you come back in five minutes."

Mike waved to his brother and left the room with a nurse. In the hallway, the nurse asked him to follow her. She was a small Asian woman with very narrow hips. She made Mike nervous with her small quick steps. He feared she was going to wait in the hallway with him, but instead she led him to a room that looked into his brother's room through a two-way mirror. He could hear what Lyle was saying.

"If our parents hadn't been such heavy sleepers—it was Ambien and whiskey—then they might have caught him. But they couldn't. Brother arsonist, he torched the piano."

The doctor asked Lyle how it had been earlier that night between their mother and father, but Lyle ignored him and kept talking about the brother. He couldn't really be talking about me, Mike thought, but then he didn't know. These were the moments that became most frightening to Mike. The strange things Lyle said didn't scare him. It was the way he ignored people, the way he didn't listen, didn't acknowledge questions. The way he could make you think that what was wrong with him was wrong with you.

Lyle spoke to the doctor in an even voice, but Mike could tell that he was becoming agitated. The doctor was asking Lyle about the third brother again. Mike watched Lyle gesticulate with his bandaged arms. That must hurt his arms, Mike thought, as Lyle made great sweeping points.

"He danced around the piano after he set it on fire. Sang around it," said Lyle. And then, confiding in the doctor, sotto voce, "He is not joyless."

"You think he sang a song, as he burned down the house?" asked the doctor.

"Not some war song," said Lyle, "something melancholy."

Lyle began to gesture violently, like he was conducting a choir. The doctor asked him to calm down but Lyle would not listen. Mike could see what was going to happen and felt ashamed that he was relieved: Lyle would be too agitated for the visit.

"He's brilliant, of course he's brilliant," said Lyle. "He sings 'Amazing Grace' instead of some war song and you all think he's OK but he's not, and if he could kill our parents he could kill all of us. He could kill you."

"Lyle, if you don't calm down I'm leaving," said the doctor.

"There has to be a manhunt," Lyle insisted.

"Lyle, you'll hurt your arms."

"He burned down the house without hesitation, without shame, like he was righteously commissioned."

Again the doctor told Lyle to calm down but Lyle kept waving his arms and the IV pole was swinging. An orderly hurried into the room and Lyle strained against him in his hospital gown as the doctor injected something into the IV.

Through the glass, Mike watched his brother lose consciousness.

The doctor appeared next to Mike and together they watched the nurses rebandage where Lyle had ripped off his dressings. Lyle's arms and part of his upper back were burned from the fire. His hair, too. The burns still glistened red and wet and raw. He looks like a baby, thought Mike, with his hair all gone.

"He insists you have another brother," said the doctor.

The doctor said most post-traumatic stress patients recover. "You can't erase the past," he said, "but you can live with it." He said Lyle would go back to school. He would get better.

There was one question Mike wanted to ask. He wanted to ask it every day thereafter, but at that moment it wasn't the right question. Mike felt it would be like a child asking for a toy, bothering a parent, when there was nothing left to talk about. *When?*

62

Mike wants to get downtown as fast as he can. He tries to hail a cab, but there are few, and fewer still stopping. Mike usually has no problem getting cabs. Jane says this is because he has good cab karma. Not today.

Jane is downtown too, or is supposed to be because it's Tuesday, one of the two days a week she works in a new clothing boutique in Soho. They joke about it, because the store is so trendy and Jane isn't trendy at all. Mike remembers clearly what she looked like the day of their high school graduation. She looked comfortable and calm in her red robe and very expensive shoes, high heels, which were unusual for her. No makeup. He remembers a cool glow about her, as everyone else sat giddy and sweating in the unexpected June heat. He and Jane have been together since they were both sixteen, but it still hasn't gotten old. And they survived being apart for a year when they were at different universities and away for the summer. Now Mike is at Columbia, too.

Jane has very white skin and is all bones, like a straw folded up into right angles, like she might blow away. Mike thinks about how he can trace the tendons in her arms all the way down to her fingers and how this disgusts him when he is displeased with her. She'll be a weird old lady. Her eyes are beautiful though. I mean, come on, he would say to Lyle if he was drunk and sentimental, she's got those eyes. She went to the funeral. One time she borrowed her parents' car and drove to Pine Hill to see Lyle by herself before Mike got home. At other times she walked the grounds while Mike visited him. For a while she was the only person Mike could talk to. Though he never told her about Tweety.

As he continues to look for a cab, Mike tries to call Jane.

NO NETWORK.

Mike glances at the cathedral. A crowd is standing on the steps and more are approaching. People are gathering. This makes sense to him. It's what cathedrals are for. It looks almost like a Sunday, but after the service.

Mike finally waves a cab down. "I'm going to Duane Street," he says, getting in. The license reads "Rossi, Joseph," a tiny, balding guy. Mike is glad he's Italian, no language problems, maybe.

"I ain't going down there. I got a police scanner in my ear. It's bad."

"I'll pay you double."

"I got a cousin in the fire department."

"Any new news?" Mike nods at the radio, which is chattering, but nothing new since the plane hit the tower.

"No," says the cabby.

"My brother's down there too."

"God protect all of them," says the cabby, "but I ain't going."

63

Mike didn't have many good days when he returned from Asia. He missed his parents. He wasn't consumed by his grief but he was quieted by it, and he didn't enjoy the things he did. His days in Bangkok were like the passing thoughts that come on the subway or in a cab, there for a moment, then gone.

One night, though, he and Jane had a bottle of wine and watched a movie and laughed and for that one evening it was like before his parents died. After they had sex, Mike went right to sleep, which was unusual. Jane went to sleep next to him wondering if they might actually get married. It was absurd, college couples getting married. But then she thought, Well, kids at regular colleges do it, just not at fancy ones. Who knows? And she slid into sleep.

That night Mike dreamed that he was back in Thailand and that he was fucking Tweety. She was back from the dead or had never died and he was fucking her against a wall in Burton's apartment.

64

Mike is out of the cab, on the street again. He still can't see any smoke. He wishes he had talked the cab driver into taking him at least a little ways downtown. Eighty-sixth Street, maybe.

Mike stops at a bodega for cigarettes, with the intention not to smoke them now but to take them downtown. He sees the second plane hit live on the tiny TV the owner is watching on the counter. He pays for the cigarettes and chain-smokes three of them before he finds another cab.

The driver is a man in a turban with a name Mike doesn't know how to pronounce.

"I'm going downtown."

"How far, sir?" the driver says, in colonial English.

"Could you take me to Duane and Elk Street?"

"Yes, no problem. Bad day today."

Mike is suspicious. "Anything new on the radio?"

"Yes, I think this will be war."

They listen to the BBC. Nobody knows anything.

"That's why I want to go down there, sir," says the cab-driver. "I want to see what happened for myself."

After that they ride in silence until Eighty-first Street, where they catch a red light. The driver looks back through the partition.

"Since you know my name, may I know yours?"

"Lyle," Mike lies.

"Why do you want to go down into the trouble?"

"My brother is there."

There is a traffic jam at Seventy-second and Broadway. Horns blast and the pedestrians hurry between the cars. Mike sits impatiently in the back of the cab. The rising heat is stifling.

On the northwest corner, a pockmarked black man in ripped jeans is selling surgical masks out of a cardboard box. He is wearing one, tied behind his fro.

"Do you think there could be some kind of disease?" the driver asks Mike, nervously, over the partition. "From the bomb?"

"It was a plane," Mike says.

"Yes, you are right. Disease would be the worst, though. There is not a good health plan for taxi drivers."

"Yeah, I know," says Mike, though he does not.

His father had managed a hedge fund and there had always been plenty of money. It all went to him and Lyle. Mike could live well for the rest of his life—and health care wouldn't be a problem. The only problem had been sorting it all out after the fire, but there were money guys who worked with his father, and they were OK. One accountant in particular, an old family friend, helped them sell the apartment on the Upper East Side, organized the money into trusts so they had enough every month, and invested the rest for whenever they might need or want it. Any reservations Mike had about wealth died with his parents.

It is getting hotter in the backseat. Mike sneezes from the heat and the driver closes the partition.

"Excuse me," they both say.

Mike's phone rings. It's Jane, but he can barely hear her voice and then the call dies. He wonders where she is. The number was her cell phone, so maybe she is on the way home. He tries to call her back.

NO NETWORK.

Traffic is moving again. As the light at Seventy-second Street turns back to red, one last cab tries to run through. It doesn't make it and swerves to avoid hitting a crosstown bus. The bus horn blasts. The cab runs up onto the sidewalk, striking a thin, middle-aged man in running clothes. When Mike sees this, he thinks he hears the man's legs crack, like a tree branch. The cab rams a pay phone and stops, smoking.

65

"You know, if that's the only way he's crazy that's not so bad," Jane said.

They were in the back of a dive off Second Avenue. It was a place that had served them in high school. Now that Mike had transferred to Columbia and they were together all the time, being here was sort of like high school again.

"Like some kind of fucked-up time machine," Mike said.

"Could be a lot less interesting," she said.

Before Mike went to Asia, he had been on a kick about how they all had to live the most interesting lives they could. Their joke was that Lyle had become too interesting. Now she was mocking him, and he frowned at her.

"He's not going to kill himself," she said.

"He'll just do what he'll do," he said. "What will happen to him will happen, is all."

"That's pretty selfish," said Jane.

"I just wish he would stop apologizing for being crazy all the time," said Mike. "How selfish is that?"

66

The reality of the accident that Mike sees at Seventy-second and Broadway is awful and surprising. The struck man is crying and Mike can see blood staining his pants. No one is going near him. Mike takes out his cell phone to call 911 but NO NETWORK.

Mike tells the driver to wait and gets out to help. He is the only one.

The quiet of the accident evaporates as quickly as it appeared. Cars rush past as Mike leans over the man on the ground.

"Help me," the man pleads, looking up at Mike, who now sees splinters of bone poking out of the man's calf.

"Don't worry."

"Don't leave."

"I'm just going to call nine-one-one."

Mike walks around the smoking cab. He looks in the window and sees the driver unconscious, his nose bloody and bent, a turban fallen off to reveal long gray hair. A heart attack, maybe, Mike thinks.

The receiver is hanging off the cradle. Mike picks it up, taps for a dial tone, and calls 911. Busy signal. Mike tries again but nothing this time, not even a dial tone. He's thinking that he will have to leave the man on the sidewalk without help. Busy signal again.

Mike looks up and down the street. Where are the cops? Mike catches himself thinking the cliché: always there when you're a sixteen-year-old smoking a joint, never there when you . . . They're all downtown. *Lyle.*

A burly guy with short brown hair and an open-collared shirt is now kneeling over the injured man. He looks like the doctor Mike and Lyle went to as little boys. Mike hopes.

"I'm a doctor," he says to Mike. "Did you call an ambulance?"

"I couldn't get through," Mike says, thinking he is free again.

"Keep trying, I'll stay with him."

"I have to get downtown, my brother's down there."

"Everybody's brother is down there. Call for this guy."

67

They sold the East Side apartment at the end of that awful summer. The last thing either of them wanted was to live with ghosts.

They both wanted it simple. Mike had transferred to Columbia so he could take care of Lyle and was living in the dorm. Lyle was living in a rented one-bedroom on Duane Street. They agreed they'd get their own bigger place together later. Mike helped Lyle move in on a Saturday morning.

The apartment was furnished and there were strange, bad paintings of animals on the walls. Five of them, all in oil. The largest was of a chimpanzee smoking a cigarette, and almost as big was a painting of a brown bear roaring out at the viewer. The three smallest were a set, all of dogs in military uniforms— a general, an admiral, and a fighter pilot. To Mike, they seemed to be looking at one another from the various walls where they hung, sharing some stupid private joke about whoever was living there. They'll keep me company, Lyle told him when he mentioned it.

Mike ignored this and kept unpacking. Lyle apologized again for being crazy.

"No, it's all right," said Mike. "We have to have a sense of humor."

68

Mike takes off running away from the accident. The blocks fall away. Running helps him gather his thoughts. Lyle never understood that. Finally, at Sixty-sixth Street, he slows to a walk. Passing a newsstand, he looks at the tabloids and learns that Mick Jagger and his daughter, Elizabeth, caused a scene at a Fashion Week party. Also, Mayor Giuliani snubbed an important rabbi. Newspapers are strange and sad and stupid things on the day of a disaster, thinks Mike.

At Broadway and Sixty-fourth Street, Mike looks for a cab again. There are more and more people on the street and fewer cabs. He can see small clusters of people watching television in pizza joints and coffee shops, sharing speculations.

Mike, too, wants to know exactly what is happening. But he doesn't stop moving. He decides he'll find out more when he gets farther downtown. He's going no matter what.

Few people are walking his way. He thinks of all the times he has walked down Broadway. Going to the movies. Going to concerts at Lincoln Center. Mike speculates on the political ramifications of the attack, but only briefly. He is sure, however, that Lyle is thinking politics, streamlining his conspiracies. Mike has grown less interested in politics as his brother has become more paranoid.

The buses running uptown are packed long before they get to Sixty-fourth Street, the frightened passengers are a collage of heads and shoulders through the windows as Mike watches them go by. At a crowded bus stop, Mike sees an older woman, probably in her seventies, talking to a little white dog she is cradling in a canvas bag. He is sure he has seen her before. That's the way it is in cities, he thinks. You see the same people again and again. It's not a mystery, only the probability of routine.

As he walks by, Mike hears the woman reassuring the dog, telling it that they will be safe, that they will be home soon and have some nice doggie snacks and watch some television. Mike thinks about his father, who also spoke to animals. Actually, his father spoke to animals and children the same way, as if it made him a better man to get down on his hands and knees and bark or ask a four-year-old how he was doing at college. Jane found this hilarious and endearing. Mike never found it that funny.

Mike remembers the woman now. He remembers seeing her and her dog one morning, about a month after Lyle moved to Duane Street. It was a bad morning. Mike had spent the night with Jane at her parents' apartment and had gotten an early call on his cell from his brother. Lyle was not doing well. He hadn't been going to classes and hadn't slept in several days—kept awake by terrible dreams. He hadn't been out of the apartment.

He said, cryptically, that there were too many conversations in his head. Bullshit movie line, Mike thought, but said he'd get downtown as soon as he could. And the woman and her dog had stolen the first cab he hailed.

Mike hadn't been to see Lyle in more than a week, and that was part of the problem. Another lesson learned.

The shades were drawn and the apartment smelled vaguely of cigarette smoke. There were piles of unwashed clothing on the floor. All the dishes were dirty and Lyle had been stubbing his cigarettes out in the sink. The television flashed silently.

Lyle had gone to sleep in his boxer shorts on top of the unmade bed. His brother wasn't heavy when he was a kid, or even before Mike went to Asia. He was always big, bigger than Mike, even, and framed in healthy musculature from a short lifetime of athletics. But in the last year he had become fat. This, almost more than anything else, was heartbreaking for Mike, to see his once lean and graceful brother perspire as he walked up stairs or breathe heavily as he ate. Lyle didn't seem to care at all. His face remained lean, though, his square chin independent of his neck.

Mike threw a comforter over him, pulled the shades, and began to clean the apartment. Cleaning made Mike feel better, gave him a sense of progress, or change at least. Lyle was getting some sleep and the dishes were getting done. It might have been a bad couple nights, bad dreams, but when Lyle woke up they would march on. If this is it, thought Mike as he scrubbed dishes, then I can handle it. Mike thought he would go grocery shopping, too, and fill the refrigerator with good food. Mozzarella and olives and roast chicken from that gourmet delicatessen on the corner. There's no reason, he thought, to live so badly.

But as he cleaned the living room and kitchen, it seemed to Mike that something was different. Something was missing, maybe. He couldn't tell what. Putting the books back on their shelves he realized what it was. The paintings were down; the strange animal portraits, the bear and the dogs and the monkey smoking a cigarette were gone from the walls. Odd, Mike thought. And why hadn't he noticed? He wondered what Lyle had done with them but then found them in the bathroom where they were submerged facedown in a full bathtub. He pulled them out, one by one, leaning them against the wall to dry. He knew that Lyle had tried to mute their voices by drowning them.

When the apartment was clean, Mike sat and watched his brother sleep. He lit a cigarette and thought about how much better Lyle looked asleep, even as fat as he was, how much he resembled his old self. Mike also saw that his brother was developing his first wrinkles, the first subtle creases of age. Good, thought Mike, at that moment. We'll both be adults and this will all get easier.

When Lyle finally opened his eyes, Mike asked how he felt. Lyle said he felt great.

Mike hears the woman's dog barking behind him as he passes the bus stop. The dog is loud and shrill and, Mike thinks, not reassured.

69

Finally, Mike is in Midtown. No cabs. At Fifty-ninth Street he turns east off Columbus Circle toward Central Park South. An enormous skyscraper is under construction and it casts a shadow on the traffic. Looking down Eighth Avenue, Mike can see more smoke rising.

When he is on Central Park South, Mike can't see the smoke anymore. The avenue is desolate and seems new and strange to him. This is where Jane lives with her parents, where she grew up, playing on the carpet and peering out over the carved paneling, through the giant windows onto the green bloom of Central Park. The apartment is beautiful and detailed, filled with art and light. Mike has a key and is always welcome. Part of the family, Jane's mother told him in tears, following the death of his parents.

Mike remembers sitting by one of the giant windows in the winter, in the middle of the night, smoking. He stared out into the dark over the bright white of the snow-covered park. Jane's parents were away in Nantucket, and Jane was downstairs picking up a pizza delivery.

Mike was wishing he hadn't slept with Tweety. Somehow that made it all his fault. The hell it did, he thought. But then the hell it didn't. It just would have all been cleaner. He wondered, for the first time, what happened to Tweety's body after she was killed. Then he heard the door open, and Jane came in with the pizza and turned on the radio. She turned the dial from the traffic report to classical music and sat down.

"You all right?" she asked, brushing her knuckle under his eye.

"Contact lenses are fucked up," he said.

"I was thinking about what we were talking about," she said.

"Which?"

"About Lyle. How he's probably alone all the time."

Mike didn't say anything.

"I have a girlfriend he should meet. We should all get drunk together. It'd be fun."

"Don't try to set him up."

"Having a girlfriend would make him feel normal."

"Having a girlfriend won't help."

Jane was silent after that.

Mike walks into the lobby of Jane's building and the doorman tells him she's not there. None of them is.

"One of the towers just collapsed," the doorman tells him. "It just fell down."

70

Outside, two Hansom cabs sit in their usual place on the park side of Central Park South. Mike wonders what they are still doing there. One driver, in top hat, vest, and sunglasses, stands between the carriages, waiting nervously with the oblivious horses.

"Still giving rides?" Mike asks.

"I'd be out of here but I told this other driver I'd watch his rig until he came back." The man's voice is a surprisingly high tenor.

"How long you been waiting?"

"Since right after the second plane hit."

Mike nods, remembering the second plane on the tiny TV screen in the bodega.

The driver whistles over Mike's shoulder at another man in a top hat jogging across the street. "Took him long enough," says the driver. "You still want a ride?"

It won't save much time, but Mike is glad for the ride across Central Park South. He climbs up into the back of the carriage, but the driver tells him to come and sit up in the front. Mike sits next to him and the driver takes off his hat and tosses it in the back. The driver is silent and grim, and the avenue is empty. The only sound he hears is the clip-clop of the horse's hooves against the distant wail of sirens.

Mike gets out at the statue of William Tecumseh Sherman across the street from the Plaza Hotel. He looks up Fifth Avenue as the cab turns into the park. Last year at this time, he and Jane took long walks up there, kicking the dry leaves as they went. There was very little rain that fall, and the summer, hot and brown, lasted through to the Thanksgiving dinner that Mike ate with her family. Lyle was still in the hospital.

As he had been taught, Mike walked on the street side of Jane. His mother had explained that this is what gentlemen did so that if a car or wild horse and buggy swerved from the street, the gentleman would take the blow, protecting the lady. Mike remembers walking up Fifth Avenue and brushing hands with Jane, and turning down the wide steps into the park at the zoo.

They walked through the aviary that smelled of green steam and bird shit, and watched the zookeepers throw fish to the sea lions. Mike remembered how, at Burton's house in Bangkok, Bridget had told him about the monotony of her father's life as a zookeeper. He didn't mention this to Jane. Instead he talked about classes and people they knew at school. By the time they were halfway through the zoo, Mike couldn't think of anything more to say, and only Jane spoke as they walked through the snake house.

Their walks helped Mike relax, but Jane would sometimes press him about *the way you've been recently,* and one day this provoked such a fierce demand for silence that she never raised the issue again. He had turned to face her so suddenly that she was briefly afraid that he would hit her. Then, blocks later, he had hugged her so tightly she had to ask him to let go. That's when he apologized, and told her that their walks were not supposed to be mental health summits.

Mike turns down Fifth Avenue and sees the smoke thickening in the sky. He sees that the city is shutting down. He notices two well-dressed men, not bums at all, passing a bottle at the foot of the Sherman statue. One of them is reading the plaque that tells that Sherman died on Valentine's Day, 1891, and the other is looking at the sky as they take turns drinking.

71

Mike is passing the expensive shops on Fifth Avenue. The window mannequins stare out at him. Jane told him once that if women were as thin as mannequins, they'd be too thin to menstruate. Jane was that thin. So was her friend Sarah, the one she thought should be Lyle's girlfriend.

Mike remembers Sarah wearing red lipstick when Jane brought her down to Lyle's apartment. The four of them sat around the card table Jane had brought as a housewarming gift. Mike knew that Jane liked the idea of routine, that they might play cards again, that it might become comfortable and regular. They had meant to play poker but instead ended up playing a drinking game called kings.

In the game, each card meant something different. The rules usually rhymed, so you could remember them when you were drunk. The rules were fluid. Jane drew an eight. "Pick a mate," she said, and pointed at Mike. She and Mike drank.

Lyle's turn. He drew a six. "Dicks," he said. He and Mike drank.

Mike's turn. He drew. "Four," he said. "Whores drink."
Sarah and Jane drank.

"What's a nine?" Sarah said, drawing.

"Perfect," said Jane, pointing to the brothers. "Nine, bust
a rhyme. They never miss. First one to mess up the rhyme has
to drink."

"OK," said Sarah, in a singsong voice. "I need some more
booze."

"Gin or bourbon, you have to choose," continued Jane.

"Lucky I can rhyme on a dime or I'd lose," said Lyle.

"I feel like I'm on a lyrical cruise," said Mike.

"Larry, Curly, and Moe were each a stooge," said Sarah,
laughing.

"OK," said Jane, "Fuck with me and I'll give you a bruise."

"Y'all," said Lyle without hesitation, "playing with you's like
takin' a snooze."

"Better watch out Lyle," said Mike, who was deliberately
the drunkest, "or you'll hang yourself in a lyrical noose."

"Drink!" shouted Sarah and Jane. "Doesn't rhyme!"

"Yeah," said Lyle, "it doesn't rhyme. Not very lyrical news."

72

Mike sees a crowd gathered on the steps of St. Patrick's Cathedral, bigger than the one up at St. John the Divine. But this crowd doesn't look like Sunday after the service. By now, they know too much.

Usually there are tourists, tentatively picking their way up the steps to walk a lap in the church. Not today. Almost everyone is going home. Mike imagines that those who linger have no home to go to. But maybe they do and there's just more comfort to be taken from sitting on the cathedral steps in midtown.

Mike remembers sitting there with Lyle. They sat on the steps and stoops of Manhattan so many times. It was one of the primary activities of childhood and then high school. He and Lyle were so comfortable doing it that once they fell asleep, sober, on the steps of the Metropolitan Museum of Art. When they woke up at sunrise they were both surprised and happy. It felt like a victory, some ascension to a higher plane of city living.

Of course, their mother told them that public places were the province of the crazy and the lonely and the poor. After they graduated high school, Mike and Lyle never hung around in public places anymore. But now, passing St. Patrick's, Mike thinks it might be good to stop there with Lyle, on their way back uptown.

73

The first time Mike actually spoke with Lyle after the house burned down, Lyle had been angry and told him that he would find their third brother and make it right. Bring him to his senses, get him off the drugs. This was during Mike's second visit to Pine Hill, with Jane waiting outside the room.

"And can't you get me out of here, Mike?" Lyle said. "I mean, you know I didn't do it."

Mike was confused by this. But he told Lyle that everything would be OK, that it would all be better soon enough. He would get Lyle out.

"Good, Mike." Suddenly Lyle's anger was gone and in its place an almost blank sadness appeared. Mike had to turn away.

Good, Mike.

74

Mike sees a man pointing his bulky cell phone at the sky and realizes he is photographing the smoke. If it were two years ago, Mike would have wanted to take pictures too. He wanted to be a photographer for what seemed like his whole life, until he went to college. He remembers his first camera and the Christmas morning he got it, during the winter that the snow was so thick and heavy it was like fiberglass. It was the one Christmas morning there was no argument. The boys had raced down the stairs at the beach house hoping their parents would be in good spirits and for once they were. They sat next to each other in front of the fire drinking coffee and watching the boys tear through wrapping. Mike received a camera from Margaret Burke White. Lyle received a guitar from Robert Johnson. The cards on the gifts were never signed Mom or Dad or Santa.

Mike photographed the whole morning. The first half of the roll was devoted to Lyle playing his new guitar. In the frames that came later, Mike's attention shifted to their parents. Candid shots of their mother giving their father an expensive shoe horn and a silver watch. And then pictures of their father pulling a long box out from under the couch. Finally, a picture of their mother grinning and sighting down the barrel of her new rifle.

"It's exactly right," she said, cocking the Winchester. "Just the noise will scare anyone off. I don't even need bullets."

"No," his father said, "if you have a gun, you should have bullets. Look in your stocking."

Their mother had been complaining that sometimes when she was home alone she was afraid the house would be broken into. "Intruders, beware," she said, reaching into the stocking and retrieving the box of cartridges.

Mike thought she wasn't afraid at all, that she only said this to make their father feel guilty for going out.

The last shot on the roll was of Mike's mother aiming the rifle into the camera. Mike thinks he'd like to see those photographs again but they were all burned up in the fire.

75

Mike's father carried a silver flask and Mike grew up thinking it was not an outlandish thing to do. Engraved on the flask were his father's initials, which were also Lyle's initials. Lyle, oddly, had the flask on him when he ran out of the burning house. It traveled to Pine Hill as his sole personal effect. Mike was surprised when Lyle took it out of the bedside table in the hospital.

Mike was visiting less and less because they expected Lyle to be released soon. It was a cold afternoon and rain fell in sheets along the windows.

"I said I didn't want it when he gave it to me," said Lyle.

"He gave it to you?" Mike was surprised again.

"Just before the fire."

"Strange."

"I said he ought to give it to you when you got back."

"Wrong initials," Mike said. He was turning the small burnished flask over in his hands.

"He said it didn't matter."

Their father, after he took a swig, would twist the cap back onto the flask and return it to his pocket, and then would brush his hands together, as if he were dusting off a day's worth of work. But the brothers rarely saw this. Their father was careful about not drinking from it in front of them. Mike didn't know if their mother had known about the flask at all. Lyle said she knew. *They were in on everything together.*

Mike and Lyle looked out the window at the rain together, thinking about their parents. The grounds were very well kept, and beyond Lyle's window they could see New England woods, darker for the rain. Mike tried to hand the flask back, but Lyle wouldn't take it.

"Keep it," said Lyle. "Last thing I need in here."

"He gave it to you."

"You know how a weeping willow works?" asked Lyle. "They need lots of water, so they grow close to rivers and ponds. The roots work right into the riverbed or whatever. The roots are wild. Apparently if there's a water pipe nearby they sense the water through the pipe and wrap themselves around it to suck off the moisture. Then you have to dig them up, because eventually they squeeze the pipe so hard it breaks. Or so Jeff the orderly tells me."

"This is half full," said Mike, opening the flask. "Have you been drinking this stuff?" he said, smelling it.

"Yeah. It was full when he gave it to me. No one emptied it. Hey, man, what are you doing?"

Mike was draining the rest of the booze. It went straight to his head. Then he was so angry, waiting for the car service outside the hospital, he didn't even notice the rain.

76

Mike stops in front of an electronics store just above Union Square. The store's sign reads HOME ENTERTAINMENT, SECURITY, COUNTERINTELLIGENCE. In the window are twenty flat-screen televisions. Some are tuned to the news, and some are tuned to cameras pointed at the sidewalk in front of the store. Mike can see himself on some of them, looking in the window, watching the news.

Mike sees footage of the second tower collapsing on one of the screens. He can't hear the narration but the images are clear. Both towers have now fallen. Lower Manhattan is lost in gray smoke. It looks to Mike like a volcano has erupted.

77

Lyle did not always believe in his third brother.

One night when Lyle knew absolutely that there was no third brother, he and Mike were out eating sushi at a place on Twelfth Street. Mike felt relieved that Lyle wasn't paranoid, that he didn't have *switch moods,* as the doctor called them, because Mike was in a dark mood himself. Sociology seminar that day had been about prostitutes. The other students had talked about problems of inherited hierarchy and gender as a social construction. About how prostitution was evidence for such things. Mike hadn't said a word.

Lyle asked him what he was thinking about. Mike told him about the seminar.

"You ever in touch with those people in Bangkok?" asked Lyle.

"No," said Mike.

"Think you ever will be?"

"I don't know."

They ate in silence. Mike broke it. He wondered if maybe Lyle could help him for once. Or if they could help each other, just by talking.

"So what does he look like, when he comes?" he asked Lyle.

"Who?"

"Our other brother."

"Fine. I'll tell you," Lyle said, and went on about the third brother. He told Mike about the visceral hate he felt for him, unlike anything he'd ever felt for anybody. About how he was witty, funny, made jokes about what else he was going to burn down. About how he had startling eyes. About how he's not superhuman but could run faster than even you, Mike, fastest white kid in the city. About how he looked like *us*.

Mike was sorry he asked.

78

Stepping into a deli in the West Village, Mike wonders suddenly what he is doing. "Why am I going down there?" he says out loud, and a short Hispanic guy next to him says, "Don't know, man."

Mike has stopped in the deli to buy a bar of chocolate, for energy, to speed up his walk. He realized how tired he was after he had to slip through a police barricade at Fourteenth Street. It looked like too many cops at Union Square, so he had walked to Seventh Avenue, where there were fewer. Mike figured out that they could only stop the people who listened to them. He just stuck to the edge of the crowd and walked by as the cops were shouting something about "identification necessary to go farther south at this time." A block later he had to rest, something that never happened to him. Fewer than three hours have passed since he stood in front of St. John the Divine, but he is exhausted. For a moment Mike considers turning around and going back uptown. He could find Jane. They could go to sleep. Maybe Lyle would be fine.

*   *   *

The white guy next to Mike is angry. He listens, with the deli guys, to the radio behind the counter.

"They're making chumps out of us," he says, jabbing a finger in the air.

"Who?" asks one of the deli guys, handing Mike change from the chocolate bar.

"The Arabs. They want to fight, they should come to Yonkers and kiss my Irish ass."

I don't want to be a chump, either, Mike thinks, looking at the white guy. Anything not to be a chump. Anything to have dignity, to look at the world slowly and thoughtfully. The most important thing is to be thoughtful. Mike doesn't want to talk to himself but that's exactly what he's doing.

"I shouldn't have fucked Tweety." He doesn't notice that everyone in the place is looking at him.

"You OK, man?" The Dominican guy squeezes his arm, snaps him out of it. Mike is embarrassed. Am I really that tired? he wonders.

He remembers something stupid he said in Bangkok, about how he was the fastest white kid in the city. It wasn't a big deal, really, but he had won the one-ten high hurdles his junior year at the city meet. Most of his friends thought this was funny and it became a joke. It was really about not being afraid of black kids. Lyle thought it was racist. All I want now, Mike thinks, is to slow down.

79

The streets are frenzied.

Mike is walking down Seventh Avenue, into the cloud where soot and ash hang in the air. The people he sees coming out are covered in yellow dust.

At Twelfth Street the intersection has become a triage center. There are lines of people. He overhears one woman say something his mother used to say, about there being two kinds of people in the world when they're standing on the edge of a cliff: one afraid of falling, and the other afraid of jumping.

A loud van passes, exhaust popping, in the stream of fire trucks. On the side of the van is a message painted in red: THANK YOU JESUS—THE CIA. What is that about? Mike wonders. He crosses the street to where a fireman is disciplining a dalmatian that won't stop barking. Mike is surprised by how violently the fireman is yelling at the dog, and even more so by the red spots of blood splattered on the black and white of the dalmatian's coat.

*   *   *

Mike's telephone rings, and he hears Jane's voice. They're both glad one of them finally got through. She says that her friend Suzy was at her father's office on the eighty-ninth floor and is probably dead. Mike suddenly loves Jane for how tough she is. She asks where he is and is upset when he tells her.

"I don't understand why Lyle doesn't just walk uptown," she says.

Suddenly Mike has a call coming in from Lyle, and he tells Jane he'll find her later.

"Maybe not," she says.

80

Lyle is on Church Street, just north of the attack. Mike knew this is where he would be.

"We should help," Lyle tells him over his cell.

"Start walking uptown," Mike says. "I'll meet you."

The soot and ash are thin on the ground, but as Mike walks south it gets thicker and resembles light snow. At Murray Street, he turns east and walks along another police barricade toward his brother. He sees cops and civilians together, carrying an injured man on a piece of plywood. A woman with long, singed black hair stands dazed, holding a napkin over her mouth. A doctor in jeans is ripping his shirt to bandage a pretty young woman with blood running down her arm from a pulsing red wound at her collar. A man in a pinstripe suit is vomiting in a doorway. Worse, Mike thinks he sees body parts, like strange, horrible animals sleeping in the street.

Mike wants to help, but he has to find Lyle. He keeps walking. A fireman runs past, carrying a crying, bloody child.

Boy or girl, Mike cannot tell. He feels sick. He needs to concentrate, to keep his head, to walk.

He looks up and thinks about being one of the people up there, a young man in a cubicle. Maybe a researcher, like Mike was in Hong Kong, with nothing to do, reading the paper online. Mike imagines that he looks up and sees, like some unbelievable joke, the blunt nose of an airplane rushing toward the window. *Like a fist, like a punch in the nose, the plane would expand until the young man couldn't see anything else and would black out just as the jet noise caught up with him.*

Mike hears an ambulance rushing behind him and covers his face as it speeds by to avoid the debris flying off its roof. A cell phone lands at Mike's feet and he picks it up. Every piece of debris is specific. The phone is on and miraculously undamaged. Twenty-two missed calls, it reads. Mike scrolls through the phone book: Alee, Cindy, Dad, Harley, Jesse, John, Kit, Lucy, O'Neil, Mom, Oliver, Orla, Steve, Trina. Mike thinks about calling "Mom" or "Dad" and telling them what he found but he can't do it. He imagines a mother sitting in front of her television, calling her child's phone every fifteen minutes. She has made a pact with herself not to call more than that, because she doesn't want to tie up the networks for the emergency services and her baby was always bad about answering the phone anyway. She's OK.

Suddenly, the phone rings in his hand, startling him. He puts it on top of a mailbox and keeps walking, thinking again what it must have been like in the buildings. *The young man in his cubicle, looking out the window, is only a few yards from the terrorist in the cockpit, before they are both incinerated.* Mike imagines the terrorist looking out the windshield. *I won't be afraid to die. The building is far away and then suddenly it is very close, and he can see into the windows for an instant, see the young man surfing the Internet. On the plane the other terrorists are guarding the passengers. A child is crying back in coach, and even the terrorist with the boxcutter cannot make him stop, though he threatens the child's father. The father keeps telling the child to quiet down, just quiet down.*

Mike walks past office furniture, a swivel chair, crashed on the street. It was sucked out of the windows of the north tower. Mike remembers visiting his father's office on Wall Street with Lyle and racing down the long hallways on a swivel chair. Then just beyond the barricade, in the distance, Mike sees a crushed body, and he knows somehow that it is someone who jumped from the tower. Mike hopes this is impossible, but he also knows what he sees, and he imagines being this person. *He is on one of the top floors when the black smoke is rising through every vent and the walls are growing hot to the touch. And he decides to jump.*

In high buildings, on bridges, on the subway platform, Mike has felt the idea of jumping. It is a small thought quickly overwhelmed by the constancy of life, but there on the subway platform an uneasy thought that often struck him. *He wouldn't even have to take a step, he could just fall, like a heavy tree, timber, onto the tracks. This man felt that pull and allowed himself to fall. More than that, he jumped. That small desire, the heart of life, that ticks like a small clock in the brain, it broke somehow. The heat became too intense, and that survival core of the brain, like a smashed clock, issued forth springs and strange ringings, and the man threw himself out the window. He threw himself and flew out, out until the ground caught up with him.*

And the man, spinning through the air, couldn't tell which way was up before he landed and cracked the concrete. And while he fell there was terror, but there was also the relief of the air. Though the air was thick, as if the whole city were choked with concrete dust, it was still a relief.

The picture that would haunt Mike later is a video still of people jumping from the top of the north tower. It's a vertical shot, and the tower fills the whole frame, with only a swath of blue sky down one side. The picture contains few colors: the strange stone color of the building, the black stripes of the windows, a wisp of gray-green smoke, and the grainy blue sky. The figures falling through the air are black and look like shapes cut from that sky. Mike sometimes turned the picture on its side when he looked at it. In this way the building looks like the ground, like some great platform. The bodies look as though they are dancing through the air, executing some extreme gymnastic trick.

Mike believes that the greatest horror of that day belongs to those who jumped, who knew early that there was no hope.

81

Mike thinks he catches sight of his brother. The strange fog hangs in different shades. Sometimes it's thick and dark; other places it's a gray exhaust, approaching white. Weaving through the anarchy of victims and rescuers, Mike can't see. But then there Lyle is, smoking a cigarette.

When Mike runs over, Lyle grabs him, pounding him on the back. This is a bad sign. When they step apart, Lyle exhales a plume of smoke, almost invisible in the haze, and produces a new cigarette from behind his ear, lighting it off the old. Mike watches this silently, stricken again by how handsome he once was.

"So?" says Lyle.

"Let's get out of this," Mike says.

Lyle nods as though he were about to say the same thing, and together they turn and start uptown.

"We'll just get home and take it easy," says Mike, thinking of the woman and her dog he saw earlier. *Have some nice snacks, watch TV.*

"I'm in good shape, Mike. I'm not crazy. You were worried this was going to make me crazy but it's not."

This is not how it sounds to Mike, but he says, "I wasn't worried. I just didn't want you to be dead."

"No, of course, I have to stop second-guessing myself like that. I just thought I should say something to put you at ease because I saw this one coming. Everyone did."

But really no one did, thinks Mike.

They are walking fast, past a van on fire. Its roof is crushed by something blackened and unidentifiable. Lyle stops to watch it burn.

"This is unbelievable," he says.

"We have to get out of here," says Mike. He's getting angry and is about to grab his brother and pull him along when he looks over to the burning van. They are too close to it, Mike realizes, as it explodes with a thick, cracking sound, blowing debris and ash up into the air.

Lyle is speaking to him, saying something, mouthing frantically in the hollow ringing, and Mike looks up and sees a gray cloud floating above them. Ashes float down slowly and lightly, as so much snow in a winter twilight. Mike turns back to Lyle and sees his brother, head upturned to the sky, catching them on his tongue.

82

Mike's father visited his son at college the day after the Head of the Charles Regatta. They were walking along the road by the river. There had been masses of loitering spectators and hot food stands along the river, but now it seemed desolate. On the other side of the road some two dozen seabirds were wheeling low and fighting over the refuse from an Italian sausage stand.

As Mike and his father turned to cross, a black minivan hit two of the birds. Mike heard the pop of a breathing thing being run over by a car and saw that one of the birds had been pulled under a tire and crushed. The other one hadn't been caught the same way. The minivan had only run over one side of it, and it lay in the road, broken but breathing. It cawed silently, and looked more human than it should have. The bird could have been saying anything. This is what Mike thought, anyway.

He and his father paused, unsure of what to do. A young woman jogging past had seen what happened, too, and stopped to look. Mike and his father didn't say anything, but the young woman produced a cell phone and made a call. Mike couldn't hear what she said, but she must have thought the silently cawing bird could be helped somehow. Mike wanted to pick the creature up, but looking at his father, he realized that the bird would just fall apart.

He expected his father to say something, but he didn't. While they all stood there, it became obvious to Mike that one of the cars speeding by would hit the second bird and finish it.

Mike looked back at his father but he had already turned away and was walking toward the path along the riverbank. Mike couldn't leave; he just stood there, watching each car go by, and then he saw the one, a green pickup truck, that he knew would run over the bird. And then it did, and there was another awful pop. The girl on the phone said, "Oh my God, I can't watch this anymore."

Mike's father was standing over the bench by the river, where he had proposed to Mike's mother. It was a new bench, actually, but in the same place. As Mike approached his father started walking away. Mike followed, watching another seabird flying over the river. What he had just seen was so much more horrible, somehow, now looking at this new bird gliding in the air. He wondered if his father felt the same way.

83

Mike takes Lyle by the arm and runs him half a block north.

The ringing subsides and the crowd thins as they make their way, with Lyle panting and Mike pawing the ash from his hair and face. Now, as they slow down, Lyle is smiling, as if to tease Mike for worrying so much. Finally the sounds of the world filter back into their heads. For a moment they are both happy. They are glad that they were there, in the middle of the disaster, and survived.

"We need a break," says Mike.

"Just keep going. Don't be a *bum,*" says Lyle.

Their father's first law was *Don't be a bum,* and this reference quiets both of them as they walk uptown.

84

Home looked very strange as Mike drove up this time. What did he mean *home*? It was ashes now anyway.

He had been busy, constantly talking to doctors and the accountant friend, and taking care of Lyle. The last thing he wanted was to drive all the way out to the end of Long Island and see what was left of the house. But finally, when he got Lyle moved into his apartment, he did. He drove out and didn't tell Lyle.

The season was over and the locals were ready, after a summer of New Yorkers, for the quiet of fall. The town looked the same. It was a fishing town and a tourist town—a good place for the boys to grow up, their parents had thought. Even if they also lived in a co-op in the city and went to private school, the beach house was always really home.

Out beyond town, the low ocean scrub rushed by as he drove closer. Everything looked the same all the way to the long gravel driveway. He and Lyle remember the driveway the same way: they are lying on the backseat and can't see where they are out the windows as their father is driving them home from wherever, but they can recognize the sound of the gravel through the bottom of the car, recognize the vibration, and know they are home.

All that remained was an ash-filled concrete foundation, a hole in the ground. The house used to rise up two stories, plus a tower at one end where his parents' office was. The tower was a short staircase up from the second floor. It was a round, open room, with a view of the ocean out beyond the windows. This was where gifts were hidden in the days leading up to Christmas. It was where his parents worked at opposite ends of the same long wooden table. In the fire, Lyle had told him, the tower fell off sideways like the head of that clown punching bag they had, bending too far, reversing, and snapping off its hinges.

Mike stepped down into the hole. The ash was still thick on the ground and in drifts from the wind. He walked the perimeter of the house and was struck by how small it seemed. Behind him, he saw his own footprints. I hope there's none of Mom and Dad in this stuff, he thought, and then was sickened by his own morbid joke.

They'd had good times in the house. It was so close to the beach that they could smell the ocean. Starting when they were quite young, Mike and Lyle often cooked together over a stone barbecue pit set into the lawn. They grilled for their parents, and in the best of times they all ate together outside nearly every day. When they were older, as the sun set they would smoke and talk and have a beer and cook tuna or swordfish or steak or burgers. Lyle was more the fish cook, and Mike the meat. In the execution of a difficult burger flip Mike would hand off his cigarette to Lyle and focus his free hands over the fire.

Lyle was a great talker. He might have some new insight about modern art or the misbehavior of the medieval papacy or about anything, really. Lyle read constantly and incorporated the language and ideas of the books he read into his conversations. Some found him eccentric or pretentious, but Mike understood him, the same way Lyle understood how Mike didn't talk much. They could communicate in different ways about the same girl they had met at the market when buying the fish— whether she was smart or not, and so on. Mike had liked very much to listen to his brother talk.

Backing out of the driveway, Mike decided not to sell. He would never sell, and never build, either. Nothing would happen here. If, centuries later, archaeologists discovered the site, they would encounter it exactly as Mike left it, hear the rumble of the driveway under their tires.

Nearly home. At an intersection they stop and Lyle looks back downtown at the smoke. Mike can tell Lyle's spirits are flagging. Mike thinks about how close to death they were. He wonders if Lyle is thinking the same thing. Mike doesn't know what to say, though, so he doesn't say anything.

When they get to Lyle's apartment, Lyle says he wants to go up on the roof, get a look at where they were. Mike wants to do this too, and tentatively pats his brother on the shoulder, but Lyle shrugs him off.

"I'm not feeling that great," says Lyle.

"Want to get some water?" asks Mike.

"Later. Let's check out the view."

86

Tweety had been waiting outside. As if a lover had whispered the scene in his ear, Mike knew it was true as soon as he thought about it.

He was sitting in class one day, back home, parents dead, brother crazy, and he knew what had happened the night he fucked Tweety. She had left Burton's apartment, and she was waiting for Mike to leave too, so she could follow him to his hotel. But he never left. So she waited there in the shadows of the compound where Burton lived. She waited, and waited, and was nervous about guards for no reason and smoked cigarettes. It was a moonless, rainy night, and the compound was dark, and Tweety was a little frightened of the dark, and she had been waiting out there, nervous, while Mike had been having his last couple of beers.

She waited, until it became clear that Mike was not going to walk out of Burton's blue door. And then Mike couldn't imagine what was in her head, because she walked back through the door and fucked him, and he didn't even remember it that well.

On other roofs around Lyle's building, at various elevations, people stand watching the smoke, listening to the sirens. Mike wants to be calm. They made it this far.

"He didn't give me the flask," Lyle says. "I just took it."

"Probably better for him, anyway," Mike says.

"I might be crazy, and I'm sorry, but I have to tell you some things."

"Look, Lyle, give the third brother a rest, OK, I don't . . ."

"It's not him."

"That's right, because he doesn't exist," says Mike.

"I saw what happened, what really happened, before the fire."

"You were asleep," Mike says, hoping he's right. "You're lucky you made it out."

"I set the fire."

"You don't have to do this, Lyle. Whatever happened, we know it wasn't you, and even if it was you, it wasn't you."

"There was a reason, Mike."

"There's no reason for this."

"I was covering for them. I had to. I didn't want you to know. You're my little brother. I'm supposed to take care of you."

"Yeah, well, take a look around." Mike immediately regrets saying this.

"I have to tell you."

"Tell me what?"

Lyle is shouting now. "That there was a reason, there was a reason."

"What reason?" Mike yells back, cutting his words short. "For what?"

"She lost it, Mike, she finally lost it and she killed him."

"What are you saying?"

"And then she killed herself."

"Fuck this."

"So I covered it up."

"Do you want to be locked up again?" Mike can barely look at his older brother.

"I was protecting you."

"I don't believe you," Mike says. "I just don't believe you. Pull your shit together. I'll be right back. I'm going to get a bottle of water."

88

The house, silent and treacherous, fills Lyle's thoughts.

He was watching from the staircase. His father walked through
the front door, after fumbling with the lock. It was late. His
mother sat in blue light in his father's easy chair, before the
blinking late-night news. The rifle lay across her lap for defense
against intruders.

"You never wait up," he said.

"I always wait up."

"What's wrong?" He stood in the doorway for a long time,
looking at her. She stared at the muted images flashing on the
television. He swayed and she stared.

"What's wrong?" he said again.

"I'm afraid," she said, and then she began to cry, wiping
her tears with the back of her hand.

"Don't be," he said. "It's not you."

"You're drunk," she said.

"I know."

"You're a drunk."

She turned up the volume on the TV.

"Turn it back down," he said.

"No," she said. "You're like this all the time." She was working herself up.

"Let me get you something to help you sleep," he said.

"Do you think," she said, too softly, clutching the rifle across her lap, "that it is a good way to live, with pills to make you sleep?"

"We just have to keep going," he said.

"You're drunk." She was very loud now.

"This will all go away," he said. "It'll be OK."

"No," she screamed, and put her forehead to the cool rifle barrel on her lap and rocked in the chair.

"It went away before," he said, and walked to the chair and put his hand out to her. She screamed again and slapped him away.

"Goddammit," he said. "We can't do this again. Look at me. Let me get you something. You'll wake up Lyle."

"Him too," she said more quietly. "I've done it to him too. He'll have this awful thing."

"You haven't done anything to anyone," he said, "Lyle will be fine."

"No!" she screamed again.

"You're incoherent," he said, and turned toward the kitchen.

"No," she said, and hit his thigh with the barrel of the rifle.

"Stop it," he said. "This is it."

She was sobbing.

"I'm getting something to help you sleep," he said.

She hit herself in the forehead with the barrel of the rifle. The veins on her neck stood out like living things. Her knuckles whitened on the gun. She hit herself in the face again and again with the barrel.

"Stop it," he yelled. But she was still hitting herself with the gun. He reached to take it from her.

Lyle jumped in the air when it went off.

"No," she screamed. "No." And she was covered in blood and terrified and Lyle didn't want to see any of it anymore and she screamed again and put the barrel in her mouth and Lyle ran down the stairs but he didn't make it in time.

When Mike gets back to the roof with the water, Lyle has jumped.

PART III

Eventually, we all sustain injuries. Realizing this, Mike decided it was easier to speak to people who had never existed at all.

89

I have been away from normal life for a while, and like many people, I lost my family in the attack on New York City. My brother.

Grief is exactly that.

So what?

Grief isn't passed down, generation to generation, with the genes. Do some genes bring grief? Do they have to? Is that what families are about? Experience. Luck.

There was family mythology, but I suspect there was a different family truth. Was my great grandfather really a swaggering forty-niner, or did he just go out there and steal shit? Were all the women in my mother's family beautiful? I used to hear my father talk to my brother about his own mythology. Vietnam and how they went through joints like cigarettes. Casualties and orders and children and friendly fire, all interwoven in stupefied clouds of glassy smoke late at night. What a cliché, but there it was. The story keeps going.

What can I say. My father and mother died in a fire. And then the towers came down and my brother died. That's the truth. But what do I do with the truth? That's the problem. Everybody was dead so I went back to Harvard.

90

I like solitary places, where I can think. Who doesn't? But once you find them they're painful to lose. This happened to me because of another student, a girl.

Behind the science center are the archaeology and anthropology buildings, much older, brick gripped in vine. They are attached to the university's natural history museum. I'm taking a graduate anthropology course and thus have access to the department library and even the museum. Some of the storage rooms house artifacts, thousands of years old. Strange old skulls and flaking bits of bone, cardboard boxes of teeth on steel shelves under fluorescent lights. None of the extremely valuable remains are stored there, but there is still plenty to look at.

Sometimes I walk around the department late at night or very early in the morning, pretending to be a harried student who must examine bones for his thesis. Such students exist and I like them. They are relentless, wearing cargo pants but not fashionably, drinking coffee and smoking cigarettes all night long. Joy in the work. It seems that some of them, at least, would rather be out digging a hole in Mongolia than giving lectures or writing papers or fooling with each other in coffee shops as happens in most other departments.

I like to look at the fossil casts in the storage rooms. I often go there and handle the bones while I'm thinking. They keep the rooms at a constant cool temperature and humidity for the bones, so it is comfortable for me in my jacket. Usually I see only the occasional researcher or assistant getting samples for a class. I would handle *levallois blade points* or a replicated *homo habilis* jaw that might still scrape me if I dragged it across my forearm, or hold the tiny skull cast of some practically simian *australopithecine* of East Africa.

When the girl came in I was sitting cross-legged on the floor holding a vertebra up to my face. I can imagine how it looked— like I was kissing the bone, but I wasn't. I thought she would just go on her way even though she paused for a moment.

I liked her immediately. She was very pretty. I haven't been dating or going after girls for a long time now, since Jane, but I liked this girl. She walked along the shelves toward me and I put down the vertebra. It turned out she was looking for a particular skull that was right in front of me. I stood up and got out of her way.

We had a conversation. What are you doing here, she asked. Working, I said. Oh, she said, she didn't mean to be a bother, if she could just get to the shelf in front of me. She had been digging in Mongolia. She had been smoking cigarettes in yellow jeeps on the arid steppe with laughing archaeologists and now she was back with me in the legitimate winter of university. Although she was from Kansas and had spent some time in Mongolia, I wasn't lost in the conversation, because I was from New York and had spent some time in Thailand. You know how that works.

But then I recited part of an Amnesty International article to her as she was looking for the skull. *The government claims that only fifteen of the almost six hundred shot dead in the past three weeks were killed by the security forces, and the rest were a result of drug dealers shooting one another. The authorities are not permitting pathologists to perform autopsies and bullets are reportedly being removed from the corpses.*

She said that was awful and amazing.

What do you know about injustice?

I asked her that.

91

This is a confession: I got angry at her. She was beautiful and played it cool, but I stared at her and said can't we leave here together? You are here at three in the morning, I said, looking for bones, and I am here, and if we could just leave together and get out of here . . .

Then my apology ensued. Sorry, I've just been working too hard and now it's so late and I'm sorry. Suppose we have a coffee on Sunday morning this weekend. No, no, she had to go to church on Sunday. Maybe I'll see you again among the skulls, I called out to her back as she hurried away.

Did she really go to church? I went to church with my father twice, and such girls were not there, not that I saw. I had a brief conversation with the vertebra in my hand.

"I want that girl," I said.

Will you go to church with her?

"No."

It's not important, to believe in God or not.

"I know."

It's no longer an abstract question. If you want that girl you have to go to church.

"I can't go to church. I don't believe in church."

You can follow her on Sunday morning.

I scared away a pretty girl. I really thought I was losing it. I felt like I was high. But I picked myself up and went home. Sometimes you just talk yourself into a corner.

Just a bad night.

I never had faith, and can't imagine ever finding it. Grief is no excuse for faith. I could sooner fly than believe in anything besides the instability of the world I have lived in. And she was only a student. She was not of the haunted tribe of vertebrae. She fled with her fossil in her hand and I sat back down on the floor and dropped the vertebra I was holding.

Just a bad night.

92

I've been assigned a final paper. The course is "an examination of belief in literature." An examination of faith. I've always been good at writing papers, but this assignment is troubling, because it's serious and I have never been a serious student. I was hardly even a student this fall. I didn't talk in seminar. I should have, because I just transferred back here, but I didn't. Nothing to say. Maybe I just didn't care anymore. So I was the silent guy.

Also, I was always cold—some psychopathology at work, no doubt—so I always wore my jacket. I think not taking off my jacket made the other students uneasy. Or maybe it was the jacket itself. It's leather and has a red rising sun with Japanese characters on the back. Maybe the jacket protects me from more than the weather. I found it in a small army-navy store in the city when I was looking for a coat for the coming winter. The place was full of people looking to buy gas masks, and the proprietor was the only one working the store. He was harried and wild-eyed, and wore dog tags that jingled over his black T-shirt and camo vest. He seemed slightly ironic about selling gas masks, telling customers that the masks would make great collector's items, although these people clearly had safety in mind.

He wasn't ironic about the jacket I was buying, but he did try to snow me. He saw me trying it on and came over. It was a little small and smelled old, but I didn't care, and I liked the Japanese writing on the back.

"Yeah, that's quite a jacket," said the proprietor. "It's a kamikaze jacket."

"How's it still here?" I asked him.

"Good question." He got very serious. "The Japanese military did sell a lot of its surplus during the disarmament after the war. Some of it went to the Balkans and some into Southeast Asia, all dirt cheap. So this could have come from there. But this particular jacket was sold to me by an old man who just came in off the street. I tried to ask him about it but he only wanted to talk cash. He was asking so little for the jacket that he was thrilled when I told him what I should give him for it. He was an old Japanese guy, actually, and it makes you think he might have had the thing the whole time since the war. Great get. I was very surprised."

I thought about this. I didn't believe the story, but it was a good jacket and I bought it for three hundred dollars, which makes it either an overpriced fake or a monumental steal. What would a real kamikaze jacket be worth, anyway? At least a life. The logical conclusion to the proprietor's story is that the Japanese guy was supposed to be a kamikaze, but either the war ended before he took flight, or he was a coward and bailed. Either way the jacket would be strong medicine.

I wear it a lot. People don't seem to hassle me as much when I'm wearing it.

93

There is a man who sells newspapers in the square. He is big and black and has a wiry beard. He has a gut and wears a baseball cap and rumpled corduroy pants and a gray coat. He stands in front of the café where students sit and tries to sell them newspapers they don't want. He is homeless, or at least says he is.

His cry has made him famous in the neighborhood. "Have a heart, have a heart, have a heart." It's almost funny the way he says it. All the words slur together at high volume, "Havahodhavahodhavahodevahelp the hooaamless."

I am not sure what he is really like. I gave him a dollar for a paper the other day, the *Spare Change News,* trying to understand him better. I had just watched a girl give him her sandwich. He kept trying to shoo her away, but she kept offering the sandwich, holding it toward him. Before, when she was about half a block away, he had said in between his have-a-heart's that he was "so hongry, have a heart." I suppose she heard him and considered the sandwich she was eating as she walked to class or to a piano lesson or a lover, and maybe she decided he could use it more.

He tried to decline at first, though. He didn't want the fucking sandwich. And I even heard him say, "No I was just kidding." Was he just kidding about his hunger? Or perhaps I had missed something in his conversation with the young woman on her way to class with her piano-playing lover? And if he was just kidding, why didn't the young woman keep her sandwich? These are strange times we live in. The girl might have had anorexia and not been able to eat. In the end, though, he took the sandwich, and I approached him while he was eating it.

He was slightly more rumpled, I saw when I got close, than I had thought. He ate the sandwich very quickly. There were crumbs in his beard, stuck like little islands in the nappy darkness. I walked up to him and said, "Excuse me, could I buy a paper, please?"

He looked at me.

I held out a dollar. I had thought about the man for a long time before I did this. I felt, and still feel, as though there were some connection between us. Not actually between us, but between me and my idea of him, which is, I guess, a selfish sort of notion. In any case, I had some ideas about this man. I had never given him any change before, even though I passed him almost every day and I frequently give my change to homeless people. There was a reason for this: shortly after I transferred back up here for school, I saw him talking out of character. He was a liar, is what I knew.

When I first saw him, I thought he was sick, or slow, or something. He was stricken with a shaking loss of control. He didn't seem dangerous, just loud, although looking at him again the day of the sandwich he looked potentially very dangerous. The young woman who gave him the sandwich was petite and very pale. He dwarfed her. Anyway, in the beginning when I saw him I thought he was afflicted in some way, but then one day I saw him around the corner from the café, talking to another man. He wasn't speaking in his paper-selling voice, and he was smoking a cigarette.

Aha, I thought, and thereafter told my friends, as we were walking by him or sometimes simply over a meal, don't give any money to the guy in front of the café. They would ask why, and I would tell them what I had seen and that the guy was a hustler. I did this as if it were my job, a noble thing, as if I had been commissioned to warn people of this criminal who in fact was never a criminal, who in fact was no more a hustler than I am.

I don't know whether what happened the day of the sandwich was an epiphany or not. I think there are many kinds of epiphanies, and this could have been one, this revelation that prompted me to give the man a dollar.

Maybe it matters whether or not you pretend to be retarded. But I realized that he wasn't pretending to be retarded, he was just working. I wondered what kind of a man he must be to stand there, in such a crowded public place, and say hello to everyone like he did.

He addressed each passerby.

"Hello sir, young lady, young man," and so on. "Lucky young man," he might say, "with such a pretty lady. How'd you get such a pretty, why hello, ma'am." And some of these people smiled back, embarrassed, and some walked straight on without looking, and some listened to music in their headphones and couldn't hear, and some apologized to him, and sometimes children mocked him quietly among themselves. He stood there for hours and hours a day, every day.

He has probably seen everything that a pedestrian can do to a bum. I'm sure he wasn't surprised at all when I approached him and asked for one of his papers as he was eating his sandwich. I bet he didn't think anything of it as I handed him the dollar and he handed me the paper.

I said thanks and was off quickly but a silent transaction had taken place, too. *I bought in.*

94

Elliot Analect came to see me. He was knocking on my door. It was a big surprise but maybe it shouldn't have been. He went to school here, with my father, and was back giving a lecture. Something about freedom of the press in Southeast Asia.

"Your father and I lived in this same house," he said, "but of course you knew that." He wore a blue suit and a white scarf and stood outside my room, as if he were a relative coming to visit. He was sort of a relative. As much a relative as anybody I have left. He and my father were like brothers once, or so Analect had told me. Made me wonder why he sent me to look for Dorr, if he was that close to my father. He must have thought he was sending me on some rite of passage, something good for me. A test. But I failed.

We took a walk, and I wore my leather jacket. He talked about my parents, and I didn't say anything.

I didn't need to hear about my parents. I knew what happened to them. I wanted to know what happened in Asia after I left. I realized I didn't even know if Bishop wrote the story.

"Your father and I had a great time here," he said.

Analect told me again how great my father was, what a *good man*, and how obviously there was nothing he could say to convey how sorry he was about what had happened.

I agreed. "I appreciate it, but you're right. There's nothing to say."

It hadn't snowed for a week, and it was a warm winter morning, the snow melting. We passed the have-a-heart guy, hawking papers.

"Christopher Dorr went here, too," I said.

"With your father and me," he said. Analect seemed to know I would ask about this. Maybe he even came to talk about it, I thought. Then he asked me, "So did you see him, while you were there in Bangkok? Bishop didn't know."

"Yeah."

I didn't know what to say. I couldn't tell him that I was afraid of Dorr, though that was mostly how I felt. But given the chance I would want another shot at him, to see him again and do battle. I don't think he'd get to me anymore, and I'd like to scare the life out of him in that house on stilts. Maybe drag him into the street and balance his legs on the curb and jump on them so they'd crack like tree branches. He was just a junkie. I would put that dog out of its misery.

"He was fucked up," I said.

"How are you doing," Analect asked.

"School," I said.

"Dorr's not in Bangkok anymore."

"What happened to him?"

"I went to check myself. Burton took me to his house in Khlong Toei, but he was gone."

"So where is he?" I was suddenly annoyed.

Analect, hands in his pockets, looked off into the sky. "Probably dead." Then he turned and looked at me and I realized how disheveled I was. How tired. And something about the way he looked at me made me want to punch him in the teeth.

"Mike, you have to be careful not to get fucked up."

"What are you telling me?"

"I just thought I'd come by and see how you are doing."

Too weird for me.

It wasn't his fault. So what if he sent me to Bangkok to get high with backpackers? That didn't fuck me up. And what did he care anyway? Maybe he felt guilty about losing Dorr, so he wanted to help me. That's what I think now. We were all the same, really, weren't we?

"I have to go," I told him, and then I took off.

People who know me know my family is dead, but I wonder if the professors all know, if there is some flag attached to my folder. Sometimes I wish everyone knew and sometimes I wish no one did, especially when it comes to the professors.

There is one professor I like. I think he knows.

He is the one who assigned me this paper on faith. This paper is important somehow. Like it could make up for a bad semester, calm me down if I work hard on it. The work will save you, my father said. Which I believe, except it didn't save him.

The paper will help me talk to this professor, at least. His name is Dr. Hunt, and it would be good to have him to talk to.

I went to a concert the night Analect visited. The band was called The Square, and it was a duo of rappers. They played on the top floor of a literary magazine building. It's an old wood place, and the magazine, called the *Advocate,* comes out quarterly, I think. Mostly messy-haired people get blasted there on cheap booze.

The Square was playing Christmas music. I was in the back of the room, smoking cigarettes out the window. It's not good, but it's mostly what I do now. I just smoke cigarettes all the time. I guess I'm at more than two packs a day. I also had what the literary people were calling jungle juice, cheap vodka and Kool-Aid, in my red plastic cup. "After all," one of the editors said, "we all know that college is in the bottom of a Dixie cup."

It seemed to me that the building could catch fire any time. The wooden dance floor creaked, and everyone was smoking, even as they danced. What starts a house fire? Fire departments have a special unit for investigating the causes of a fire. Usually they don't figure it out exactly. It's usually a mystery.

A family in a house. Their lamp falls over. Somewhere behind the walls a fuse blows. Wires cross, blue sparks fly. Someone leaves the oven on. A child plays with matches. A cigarette butt ignites the trash. Maybe they forget to put the candles out after dinner, because they drink two bottles of wine and run upstairs to bed. Maybe the weather gets so hot in the summer that the house just combusts. Maybe the floor gets too hot to stand on, like the sand you have to run across at the beach in the afternoon, and then bursts into flame. A fire of undetermined origin is what the investigators call it.

The investigators know some things, though. Twenty-five and a half percent of fires start in the kitchen; 15.7 percent in the bedroom; 8.6 percent in the living room; and 8.2 percent in the chimney. About thirteen people out of every million will die in a house fire this year. The leading causes, in order, are cooking, arson, heating, and careless smoking.

The band began playing "Carol of the Bells," and the MCs started a call and response over the carol. The kids were drunk and screaming and dancing.

On, on they send on without end their joyful tone.

It was so beautiful I had to leave.

97

I should not have been so abrupt with Analect. I regret it now. I wish I had been more thoughtful. Elliot Analect wanted to make everything right. He wanted to tie up loose ends. He wanted to be decent, check in on his friend's orphaned child. He was trying to be thoughtful. I don't know what's wrong with me.

98

I went to a holiday church service. I thought I might see the archaeology girl. I thought we might run into each other on the wide, snowy steps, and she would see that I am not crazy. She would hear my singing as we all stood and sang. She would see the attention I paid, the care that beamed from my eyes for things sacred. On the way out I would apologize. Maybe something would happen.

I didn't go just for her. She wouldn't like me if I did. I went because I have always liked churches. This one is simple. New England, white, cushioned pews. Famous people give talks there. The Dalai Lama. Famous writers. People of note.

This turned out to be a fancy annual service. I had no idea. Upstanding young men in tuxedos handed out programs on heavy paper as you walked in. The chaplain stood up in the pulpit and I remember he read some of the nativity, and then gave his talk, whatever it was. There was singing after. It was a pleasant service in a dimly lit church. I didn't listen to what the chaplain talked about.

I wish I could remember. I haven't been remembering things so well. A shrink I saw in New York told me he thought my condition was *suggestive*. That is, I think I'm forgetting things; therefore I make myself forget things. For example, I made an appointment to follow up with the shrink, but I forgot when we scheduled it. I genuinely forgot, but he said it was an example of the suggestion. After that, I was too embarrassed to go back.

There were some professors at the service. A few of the old ones are religious, practicing. Most of the ones I saw had no religion but liked to have an evening in the church. I suppose that's what I was after too, even if I can't remember what the service was about. I'm not religious, but I believe in something.

I'm spiritual.

That's what everybody at this university says all the time, so I'll say it too. But fuck those people and fuck me. I didn't mean to, but I got so angry thinking about all this at the service that I walked out of my pew more forcefully than I should have. People turned, and the chaplain even had to pause because of the disturbance. At least the archaeology girl wasn't there.

Out into the snow down the wide steps.

99

The next day, Dr. Hunt came up to me in the hallway as I walked
to class. He started to make conversation. Turned out he was
at the church service and he wanted to see *how I was doing*.
He said he didn't want to pry but that I looked upset as I was
leaving the church. I tried to remember. I have this bad feeling
that there might have been tears on my cheeks when I left.

I didn't want to confide in him. What would I say, anyway. I hope I am not being willfully rude, but everybody is dead.
I don't have anything I want to talk about.

"If you ever want to talk, have a cup of coffee, here's my
phone number," he said.

"Thanks," I said, and walked off quickly, flipping the piece
of paper into a wastebasket.

I've been having this urge to make everybody afraid. I know
this sounds harsh. I want Dr. Hunt to grind his teeth the way I
do, and I want him to be afraid. I want him to walk and feel as
though someone might leap from the bushes and grab him and
beat his face in with a rock. On the first whack all his good white

teeth would break and then on the second his lips would be forced into them and would rip and tear and the blood would be everywhere.

I get so tired after I think about this, I just want to sleep for days.

That night I looked up Dr. Hunt's number and called him and set up a time to talk with him over coffee.

100

In my dream, I see Tweety executed. I think I have it a lot. I wake up too quickly and can't remember, but I think it's what I've been dreaming.

I think it happens like this:

I have eyes in the back of my head. It's too strange to describe, seeing the world in two directions. I am on the blue motorcycle behind Harrison and we are speeding away, except this time, because of these extra eyes I have, I can see behind us as we go. First the lieutenant tells them to kneel, which Tweety's brother does, but Tweety won't. She starts fighting them, and it gives me hope for a moment, but then one of the cops whips her face with the butt of his pistol. As soon as she falls down they shoot her, and then they shoot the brother, who is still kneeling and has pissed himself. My normal eyes close, as I hear the pistol shots, but these awful eyes in the back don't blink.

101

Dr. Hunt and I planned to meet at his office and then go somewhere else for coffee. I meant to arrive on time but I was late, like I've been late everywhere recently. I was reading the newspaper and got caught up in it, a story about a corrupt fire house. Practically a whole ladder company had fucked the same woman, and no one would take responsibility for the kid. When I noticed the clock, I knew I would have to run to Dr. Hunt's office to make it on time. But I had decided, the moment I walked on campus this year, not to run anywhere. It's never worth the loss of dignity to be running to class like some frazzled premed. So I walked to his office and was late.

Dr. Hunt's door was open. He's a senior professor, so his office has a window view out over the campus from the third floor of the English building. The room was full of yellow sunlight. It was midmorning and he was sitting at his desk making notes in a novel. The walls were neat bookcases and he said to please sit in the comfortable chair in the corner, not the wooden one in front of his desk.

I was burning up the whole time. I didn't know what I would tell him and I feared that I was going to break down like some fourth-grader during his parents' divorce. I was afraid that I was coming so that I could do that without meaning to. I was second-guessing my own intentions.

Dr. Hunt said we'd lucked out with such a beautiful day. I agreed. He asked me about the essay, the one I'm supposed to be writing. I told him the essay was fine, I've just been a bit of a mess.

Hunt nodded sympathetically.

I cut right to it. I knew what he was looking for. New Englander, white hair, a grandfather, an intellectual, he genuinely wanted to help. He thought that with sensible discussion and growing one's own tomatoes and crisp weather and long walks in the woods and a nice woman and study and a glass of wine, anything can be rectified.

"Yes," he said, "I noticed you seemed a little uneasy leaving the service. It's a cliché, you know, but this is a hard time of year. Gets to everyone."

"I guess you know my deal," I said to him.

"No, I just thought . . ." He's kind and forgiving and takes off his square spectacles.

"I didn't come here to spill."

"No, I just thought we might have a coffee. I quite enjoyed having you in the class."

"I didn't talk much." I couldn't believe he didn't know.

"You didn't have to," he said. "Shall we go get a coffee?"

I could have told him that I fucked a hooker and got her killed in Thailand. I could have told him my mother killed my father and then killed herself. I could have told him my brother set our house on fire. I could have told him that my brother died on 9/11 in New York. I could have told him that I was terrified, that, like original man climbing down from the trees some moony night, I was afraid my mind was betraying me and there were creatures waiting for me out there in the darkness. I could have told him that I hear a voice and see a girl carrying a baby on a motorcycle.

I was about to lie maliciously and I felt bile in my mouth and my temples tightened and I let myself get into it. Somehow it was making me feel better.

"My girlfriend was pregnant," is what I said to him, "and then she died in a motorcycle accident."

His fingers were together and his eyes closed for a moment.

I let that hang for only a second and then, as if I had the strength not to linger on it, I said, "Yeah, I've been talking to my parents and they've been taking care of me and especially my brother has been great, you know, my best friend. I just didn't feel like seeing them this break so I stayed here and maybe I shouldn't have. Maybe I'll still go home."

Kindly Dr. Hunt swallowed the whole thing. I felt better and he didn't try to tell me anything. We walked out into the cold sunshine and he bought me a coffee and we talked about books for a little while. Then we wished each other Merry Christmas and he said he was looking forward to reading my essay.

"You should go home for Christmas," he said. We shook hands.

*   *   *

The meeting reminded me of a story I heard in Hong Kong about a Japanese mailman. The guy lived in Hiroshima, and when we dropped the bomb the heat scorched the shadow right off his skin but he survived. He pulled himself out from under his destroyed house, blistered and broken, and managed to get on his bicycle. He biked for a day straight, just to get out of the radiation. He didn't stop until he got to Nagasaki, just in time to get nuked again. But again he survived. An Australian radio reporter met him in the hospital just after, when he was dying from a mutation in his blood but didn't know yet. The reporter asked him how he felt. He said he felt like the luckiest man alive. Likewise.

102

It's a tradition to piss on the statue of the university's founding father, John Harvard, in the middle of the night. The statue is a bronze, triple life-sized, stern gentleman sitting on a chair on a pedestal in the middle of campus. Boys and girls both scramble up and urinate on him.

It never occurred to me to piss on it before I left the first time. Too stupid. But the college handbook emphasizes the importance of community, and I'm back now. So why not? Plus, the archaeology girl, before I scared her off, told me to lighten up. This was my intention the night I went to uphold tradition.

The air was clear and very cold, like every night here it seems, and the water in my hair from the shower froze as I walked outside. Campus was deserted, but light shone from every window, backlighting students as they worked or drank.

Usually the pissing is done in groups and drunkenly, but I was not drunk and went alone. I might have called someone. Come with me and cheer for me, I would have said, the way they do, ironically and drunkenly, for each other. But I had no one to call, really.

The statue was like a temple, I decided, and so I treated it as such. I decided to appeal to its wisdom as I was pissing on it. Piss was the appropriate offering, and so I would offer it respectfully. It was too slippery and stupid to climb the thing, so I stood in front of it, unzipped my pants, and urinated on the base of the statue. Steam rose from the urine as it landed on the frozen metal and melted the snow below. I spoke a quiet prayer and felt like a fool as I zipped up. But nobody saw, nobody was around. I stood there for a long time with my cheeks turning colder and colder thinking about what I had learned so far at college. Everyone agrees that you don't go to college for classes. You go to make friends and connections. You go to get laid. You go so you can leave your family but not be lonely.

And then I heard people coming. Two boys and two girls. Peacoats and parkas in the cold. They were leaning on one another, laughing, and holding one another's arms. I took out a cigarette and lit it.

"Here, here," said one of them, "let it be known that Dorothy has come to enact tradition."

One of the girls seemed to be dragged along.

"Come on," said her friend, "we've all done it."

They noticed me and the loud leader boy said, "Excuse me, fellow student, another of our kind must leave her mark on the fair founder."

I nodded and backed out of the way, smoking my cigarette, but watched from close by. They paid me no attention. They were too busy convincing Dorothy to piss on the statue.

Eventually she did. I watched her climb up on the statue. She looked around nervously and her friends did, too, but no one was there but me. The girl stood on the statue's thighs and his benevolent bronze face looked out at me over her shoulder. It was an inexplicable scene, this panting little primate on the oversized bronze man.

"Turn around," she shouted at her friends, and they did.

"We're listening," they said.

The girl had forgotten about me. The truth is I was hiding and watching. She steadied herself against the statue's head, and then, like some circus chimp, crouched, and pulled down her pants. I could see, where she held back her peacoat, her spectacularly pale legs and a spot of pubic hair. Then she began to piss and the urine ran down between her legs and trickled steaming down the statue and she said, "Oh, this is freezing," and her friends laughed and said, "Sounds like a good one, Dot."

Dorothy pulled her pants back up and started to climb down, but she slipped. I thought she might smash her teeth on the bronze but she didn't. I watched her flail and then land heavily near my urine-soaked snow. She let out a short yelp of surprise and her friends were suddenly serious.

"That looked terrifying, are you sure you're OK?"

"I think so," Dot sniffled.

Let's go get some hot chocolate and *feel better,* they all agreed, and they walked away to get hot chocolate together in the cold night.

103

I also wish I could have gone with them. Part of me wanted to get some hot chocolate.

Jane and I are not together anymore. It was fucked after 9/11. I was cruel and essentially unwell for a long time, since Tweety, really, and if I can salvage something from my behavior it's that I was cruel to Jane because it wasn't good for her to be around me. So I didn't really give her a choice. This is what I tell myself.

"Maybe not," she had said over the phone on 9/11, when I said I'd find her later, and that was it. She had been fed up. After that, I didn't try to talk to her again. She called when she found out about Lyle and left a message about friends relying on each other, even if they weren't together anymore.

I was somewhere else by then, though, and never called her back. It was too late. Somewhere else, ha, like where I am now. A different city, a different college. Long-distance relationships, I have heard people say, never work.

104

Hoping to see that archaeology girl, I often went back to the Museum of Natural History. I reasoned that she was an archaeology major, so she must do research there.

The last time I was there, an elementary school class was visiting on a field trip. I was looking at the best exhibit, which is the reconstructed polar bear skeleton. I have often broken the rule and run my hand over the bones of that ancient bear. They are yellow and indescribably smooth and brilliant to the touch.

The class came by as I was looking at the bear. They were following a grad student who walked with the wide and friendly waddle of an herbivore. She wasn't the archaeology girl, but she was eloquent and informative. Polar bears are as intelligent as apes, she explained. A polar bear might travel the whole Svalbard Archipelago, or cross Canada, padding calmly over the ice to Alaska, and then walk back. Sounded like a good trip to me. I started trailing behind the class.

*   *   *

It was a particularly beautiful group of children, from some Catholic school, I think. The boys in their ties, with their thin, almost elfin complexions. Even the fat ones were not sticky or vulgar. The girls seemed older, of course, in their plaid skirts and polo shirts.

After a couple of exhibits a security guard, whom I saw all the time when I went in and out of the museum, approached me and asked me to follow him. I said sure, of course, what's the problem, and I realized that the herbivore guide was eyeing me as she was explaining about monkeys. She had called this guy when I wasn't looking. He said I wasn't supposed to follow the kids. I said I wasn't following the kids, I was just listening to the lessons. It was absurd. I had stolen a look or two at the older girls in the back but I wasn't stalking them. I didn't even care about the kids; I was just half hoping that the archaeology girl might be around.

I went with the guard and felt the kids watching my back as I left. No harm, I said, trying to make conversation. I understand, what with the terrorists and all, you have to protect the children. This seemed to make the guard clam up even more. I couldn't believe it. He saw me all the time, he saw me just coming in to look around, not causing any trouble, all the time. But now he thought I was a creep, probably a pervert criminal.

So I left the museum forever that day, which is no good, because I went there all the time. I have to start finding new places to go.

105

I knocked on Dr. Hunt's door again today. I knew it was Christmas Eve, but I thought he might be in and that we could have some friendship, some small warmth if I came clean and apologized for lying. Why did I think he would be there on Christmas Eve? When I walked across the packed snow to his office I didn't see anybody, and I didn't even see anybody on the way back to my room.

I should have prepared a letter to leave for him. Or maybe finished the paper and left that. Or I could have left this, whatever it is I am writing now, but of course I am not finished with it.

106

Walking back from Dr. Hunt's empty office, I imagined that it wasn't Christmas Eve and people were around, but everyone was frozen, suffocated under the snow. It was a very beautiful scene.

It was twilight, with snow falling. The students would have frozen as they walked, then been covered by the falling snow as it drifted around their striped sneakers and up along their jeans, until the drifts reached their peacoats and drifted up their torsos to their elbows, around their messenger bags, and up along their arms to their cell phones as their mouths were covered. The cell phones would die, and the snow would silently and slowly reach up to their eyes, and stick to their open irises. Finally they would all disappear under the snow. Only Tweety and I would be left, and we would stand in the middle of this storm and catch snowflakes on our tongues.

I am beginning to regret, now that they are frozen, the fear that I wished upon them.

107

I have this letter I've been saving:

> Dear Mike,
> I'm not dumb. I know it's time for me to get better.
> You can't be a *bum* anymore, is what Dad would have said.
> *Bums* don't get anything done. A *bum* doesn't write the
> essays. A *bum* would pretend to be sick to leave school
> and live off his charred parents.
>
> There is no justification for *bums*. They come in a
> million varieties and each one's got a different excuse.
> There's the *Sick Bum*, the *Heartbroken Bum*, the *Be-
> trayed Bum*, the *Bum Who Doesn't Care*—because he's
> an *Atheist Bum* or a *Shell-Shocked Bum* or a *Bum Who's
> Too Smart For His Own Good*. There are the *Invisible
> Bums* whom nobody notices and the *Bums Living Under-
> ground*. There're no criteria for a *bum* except that he
> doesn't do the work, and like our father said, there's
> salvation in work.

That's what *bums* don't understand, that the greatest virtue in the world is action. Not being a *bum*. I just don't know what I'm going to do about that. *Bums* drop out and don't do the work.

It's all lack of action. Inaction, that's being a *bum*. Death. Inaction. That's what I'm worried about. We're all *bums* when we're dead.

The letter was signed by Lyle and dated September 9, but I didn't find it until October.

I hope I can pull something out of this for the essay on faith. I keep getting distracted as I sit here trying to write it on Christmas Eve. I was searching the Net and I looked up Harrison. Harrison Stirrat. I have been looking at his pictures, and I wasn't prepared. The pictures are horrific. There was an old one, up on a French photo agency Web site, of a little boy holding up a pair of hands to the camera. The boy has an assault rifle hanging over his back and an oversized T-shirt down to his knees, like the kind I wore to bed when I was a little boy. He is almost waving the hands at the camera, with their bracelets of dried blood. I could just imagine Harrison, short, bald Harrison, standing in front of that kid and taking the picture, and then telling a story about it later in some bar.

What I couldn't take were Harrison's new pictures. A photo essay about the *yaa baa* life in Bangkok. They were very ordinary, actually, except for the access. Just simple pictures of stoned young Thais, and some mundane shots from inside a factory. The images looked almost serene, and seeing them made me feel like a liar. Maybe I made the whole thing up. I feel like I've been telling the same stories again and again, lying. That is part of why I was so quiet this semester. I am very tired of lying.

Lyle told me that he saw our mother kill our father and herself before the house burned down. Before he burned it down. But I don't know if I believed him. He wasn't killed in the 9/11 attack. He jumped off the roof. He killed himself. I didn't believe him and went to get water, and when I came back, he had jumped off the roof. Maybe if I had believed him it would have been different, but you're supposed to tell people the truth, right? You can't just go along with whatever lies they make up. Otherwise you can never live right.

Lyle told me he burned down the house because of what he saw. So I wouldn't have to see. I'm telling you so we won't forget. And who else could I tell? Anyway, you should know, he blamed the fire on you, *Brother*.

I'm leaving. That's what my parents would have done, and what Tweety did, and what our brother Lyle would say to do. I'm walking out through the snow to the highway just beyond campus and I am walking back into the world. I am walking across the highway, just as I am, and getting out. Even if I see a girl, holding a baby, flying down the snowy highway on her motorcycle.

I just can't believe, of all the people in the world, I'm telling this story to you.

ACKNOWLEDGMENTS

Grateful acknowledgment to: Thomas McDonell, Terry McDonell, Supattra Vimonsuknopparat, Torgeir Norling, Judy Hottensen, Morgan Entrekin, John Stauffer, Eden McDowell, Juliet Lapidos, and The Thompsons of Paumalu Place.

In memory of Tristan Egolf

Also by Nick McDonell

Twelve

Twelve is a chilling novel of urban adolescence that captured the soul of a generation and caused an international sensation. It is cool and cruel and utterly compulsive.

'Nick McDonell is the real thing… I'm afraid that he will do for his generation what I did for mine.' Hunter S. Thompson

'As fast as speed, as relentless as acid.' *New York Times*

'Bret Easton Ellis territory… an extraordinary, assured debut.' *Harpers & Queen*

'For once, the hype is all true.' *Sunday Telegraph*

'McDonell is an authentic talent and, long after the storms of hype have died away, his novel will endure as a snapshot of his generation.' *Observer*

'Consistently brilliant… One of the most exciting new writers around.' *Independent on Sunday*

'A brilliant satirical debut.' *Time Out*

'Sleek, seductive, tightens like a vice.' *Uncut*

'This compulsive elegy to wasted, privileged youth, lives up to the hype… McDonell's prose is lean, elegant and bleakly witty.' *Elle*

'A small masterpiece.' Germaine Greer, *BBC Late Review*

Atlantic Books
Fiction
ISBN 1 84354 072 X